Bob Moats

I0567407

Campground Murders

By Bob Moats

This book is a cross over between the Jim Richards series of books and the Fatal series of books.

Campground Murders

ISBN – 978-0-9960845-6-7

For information and address:
Magic 1 Productions
P.O. Box 524, Fraser MI 48026-0524
Website: http://murdernovels.com
Cover by Bob Moats

Bob Moats

Other Jim Richards series books by Bob Moats

For a preview or to purchase a book, go to
http://murdernovels.com

Campground Murders

What people are saying about the Murder Novels by Bob Moats

"I went online this morning and read your book. I thought at first that I would only read a few pages, but got sucked into it and read all 11 chapters. You are a very good writer! I read quite a bit and often pick up "Airport" paperback mysteries to read on a plane. Most of them are dreadful, with obvious plots. Classmate Murders is a much better story than most."

Ray Zink, Entrepreneur, Minn.

"I got up to chapter ten of the Classmate Murders and decided then to buy the next two books." ... "Just finished your third book, the Dominatrix Murders. I thought it was the best one of the three, didn't want to put it down till I finished it. I looked forward to seeing how Penny would greet (Jim) every day after her show. Keep the books coming can't wait for the next one."

B. Norris, Retired Naval Corpsman

"Classmate Murders is well written and keeps the reader involved and wondering what will happen next throughout the book. Showgirl Murders keeps the reader involved throughout the story and keeps you guessing as to who the murderer is until very near the end."

G. Shurig, Kalamazoo

Bob Moats

"If you like mysteries and action then don't miss reading this book..."

Jan Schneider, avid mystery/crime reader

"I finished the book last night, and really enjoyed it. I can only read a book that fast when it keeps my interest, so that should tell you a lot. I would recommend this book to others. I look forward to reading the next installment of the book."

M. K., retired Chrysler Admin.

"I haven't finished the book yet. When I enjoy a book, I take my time, but I want to buy the other two books. I compare your writing to a Mickey Spillane novel, and I like your style, very narrative. I'm amazed you don't have a publisher yet."

Michael Rasah, Professor of History

"Thanks for making me immortal, love the stories, your friend, Buck."

The real "Buck", George Carver

"Your books have been a joy to read. They keep me interested until the last page is turned. Keep up the good work!

B. Scharmann, Rochester Hills, Michigan

Extra special thanks to:

My gratitude to Sally Berneathy who edited this book and is editing some of my other books. If you need an editor for your work go to http://sallyberneathy.com for more info.

Thank you for purchasing this book. I hope you enjoy it as much as I enjoyed writing it for my faithful readers. Please feel free to email me to tell me what you thought about my stories. I can be reached at murdernovels@mail.com thanks again!

This book is a cross over between the Jim Richards series of books and the Fatal series of books.

Chapter 1

We were one day out of Las Vegas on the road north. Penny and I had decided that we wanted to see Seattle and climb the Space Needle. We had two weeks to travel out and then back to Vegas for Penny's show premiere. I figured that Seattle was close, yet far enough to enjoy the first week. Then down the coast to LA. My GPS was arguing with me most of the way up. I threw it in the back of the van and let Penny navigate.

"I think we should have turned right on that last road, Sweetie," she said.

"It would've been nice if you'd told me a little further in advance before I get us lost. There is no straight shot to Seattle from Vegas, and I'm not sure if we can make it up there and back in a week going this way. The main highway to the great Pacific Northwest runs through California. This way is a mess of highways that go north, then south, then west. We can go a couple hundred miles out of the way to California, then up. This way will take forever."

"I'm looking at the map. This way will take us to Washington State if we jog over to Reno."

Campground Murders

"Okay, how much longer?" I asked.

She took out a small ruler to measure the scale of miles, then measured the map. "When we get to Reno, it's about 750 miles straight up." She was looking at her cell phone. It had the map information. "It should take us twelve and a half hours driving straight through."

"Are you serious? I'm not driving twelve and a half hours. You want to take over, fine. I'll do six hours, you take the rest. I've had enough of the Stratosphere in Vegas. Why do we have to climb the Space Needle? Are you going to push me off that structure so I can say I've been nearly killed twice from a half mile up?"

"Silly, no. The Space Needle is a historical landmark. It was made years ago for the Seattle World's Fair. You can jump if you want, but I won't push you."

"Thank you, that's comforting to know. I'm sure you'll want to go to the original Seattle Starbucks to get a cup of coffee?"

"Of course. I'm not fond of coffee, but I want to say I've tasted it from their first store."

"I'm sure it tastes the same as from the millionth store," I said.

"Where's your sense of adventure?" she asked.

"I left it back in Fallon. We should have stopped there for directions."

"You don't need directions; I'm going to get us there. See! There's a sign saying we are heading to Reno."

"Isn't Reno where people can get a quickie divorce?"

"Never mind. We're stuck with each other. No quickie divorces for us," she replied.

"What about that death do us part thing?"

"You go ahead and jump from the Space Needle if you really want that option." She smiled.

"Okay, we're stuck with each other. I'm a coward when it comes to killing myself."

Willy came up to the front of the van and barked. I looked down at him and said, "What? You have to go now?" I looked at Penny. "See, we should have stopped in Fallon."

"Fine, pull over and let the dog relieve himself. Better than stinking up the van."

Campground Murders

I saw a small turnout in the road and pulled over. We all got out of the van and stretched our legs. Willy was put on a leash and we let him do his business.

"Does the air seem fresher out here? The air in Vegas is too dusty," I said.

"Sweetie, it sits in a desert. Of course there's more dust," Penny replied as she let the leash run out to its end. Willy scouted trees and then relieved himself.

"I can't watch the dog. It'll make me want to go, too," I said.

"You know where the toilet is. Just be sure to close the door. We are out in the public now."

"Nobody can see the toilet from outside. You just don't like looking at me on the toilet. It's good you have your own bathroom back home. You don't have to look at me taking a dump," I said with a grin.

"I may not see you but I can smell you," she said then went around the van, pulled by Willy.

"Hey, my poop don't stink," I yelled to her on the other side of the van.

"So you think. Can we talk about something else?" she yelled back.

"Fine, is Willy done sniffing every bush?"

"He's digging now. Maybe he smells treasure."

"Or a dead body," I said quietly.

"Don't you even mention dead bodies or murder at any time we are on this trip," she said, coming up behind me from around the front of the van. Willy bounced at my feet. I bent down and picked him up.

"Yes, dear, I won't mention it. You know it's been nice that my cell phone hasn't buzzed once since we left," I said.

"It's only been a day. Give Deacon time to start worrying about how to change a diaper," she said as she unhooked the leash.

"I think Lynn can help him with that."

She wound the leash and said, "You couldn't change diapers, could you?"

"No, I have a very low threshold for bad smells. Can we talk about something other than poop?" I asked.

"Well, you brought it up. Twice. Now can we get moving? It's going to get dark soon," she said and went around the other side of the van to get in.

Campground Murders

I looked at Willy in my arms and said, "Don't ever get married."

"I heard that!" came Penny's voice from the van. I swear she had radar.

I got in, dropped Willy on the floor and started up the van. "See if there's a campground or Walmart around Reno."

"Walmart?" She gave me a strange look.

"Sure, Wally World. Most of the RV people know that Walmart is friendly to us resting in their parking lots. They're smart. If we stop there for the night we will most likely buy something from them. They win, and we do, too."

"I'm not camping out in a parking lot. I want a fire and marshmallows." Penny pulled out her phone to look up campgrounds.

"I hate marshmallows," I said, turning up my nose.

"You hate everything," she replied.

"I like you."

"Don't start that again. We've been down this line of reasoning before. Okay, I found a nice small

12

RV park on the Nevada and California border. Keep on this highway until we get to Reno then north on 395. I'll guide you there."

"Now I'm sure we will get lost."

"You can do this yourself and I'll drive," she said.

"No, dear, you're doing fine. Just get us there before midnight."

"Another hour, and it's still light out."

We drove on through Reno. I didn't want to visit. I'd heard it was congested with people. It's the little Las Vegas and spa city of north Nevada. You can gamble your money away and get divorced all in one setting. We journeyed out on Interstate 395 until we got close to Border Town. That, for obvious reasons, reminded me of the Mad Max movies. I was expecting to see a bunch of makeshift vehicles roaring out of the desert, shooting my tires out, then Mel Gibson coming to our rescue.

Penny was still consulting her maps and phone, guiding our vehicle to the RV Park. It turned out to be a small, rundown campground with about ten spaces for smaller RVs. I pulled up to a house and got out. Penny came out with Willy on his leash, and he took to sniffing the bushes again.

Campground Murders

Some older man came around the house and said hello.

"Are you the campground manager?" I asked.

"Sure, if you want me to be. I own the property and let RVs camp here. It's out of the way of the city and quiet. You staying for the night or longer?" He came closer and looked to be in his eighties. Grey hair and wrinkled like a raisin.

"Just the night. We're on our way to Seattle," I replied.

"Well, that's still a ways away. You can pick any spot you want. As you can see we only have two other RVs parked. The fee is $50 per night. That includes electricity. Just hook up to the extension cord on the ground."

That worried me. I could see it wasn't the best, but it was handy. Penny came up and whispered, "I'm sleeping with my gun."

*

Chapter 2

"Well, you picked this place," I said after we parked in the space and were getting out the gear for camping the night.

"Well, the phone didn't have a rating for these places. I just picked one by how close we are to the highway. I didn't know we would end up in the RV Park from Hell," she said.

"We don't know that. This isn't a bad place. The owner seemed nice."

"I didn't get close enough to see how many teeth he had. He probably has a chain saw in the shed."

"I doubt that. I didn't see a shed," I said, staring at the extension cord on the ground, afraid to touch it. I didn't want to turn Penny into a widow so soon. I bent down and looked closely. It seemed safe. I pulled the van power cord out and hooked it up. It worked. "Now we can relax and have a bonfire."

Penny was looking around at the desert. "Where do you plan to get wood for a fire?"

Campground Murders

She had a point. "I wonder if the owner has a wood pile out back of the shed," I said with a smile.

"Shut up. I want a fire and marshmallows."

"I'll see what I can find." I left her to go to the house to see if there was any fire wood to be had. Penny was waiting, sitting on our foldout picnic table mumbling to herself when she jumped as a small boy came up behind her.

"Hey, lady, how are you? I'm here with my fambly, and I'm bored. Does you have any games to play? My fambly doesn't, and I'm bored."

After Penny's heart restarted she laughed as I came back. "Jim, this boy is looking for some games. Do you have any?"

"Sorry, I'm not into games." I looked at the boy. "Maybe you could make a game of finding fire wood for us."

Before I could explain that I was kidding, he said, "Okay," and ran off.

"That wasn't nice. The poor boy was bored and wanted us to help him."

I sat next to her and said, "Just wait until his other twelve brothers and sisters come over for a game."

"How do you know this?"

I smiled. "I counted them as I went to find the owner. Give it time. Oh, and the owner has no firewood. He suggested cactus but said it's illegal to cut them down."

Penny looked out to the desert and said, "Why? There are millions of them. It's not like they are an endangered species."

"I think he was pulling my leg. There are plenty of small trees but it would take me all night to collect enough branches from the ground."

Penny looked again to the desert and laughed. "Well, you may have your branches yet." She pointed behind me, and I turned. There were about thirteen children out gathering branches. One had even found a whole tree that was down.

About ten minutes later there was a pile of wood on the ground by our van. All the children were playing with Willy as I was trying to break up the wood. Penny was helping them to play. It was cute.

I made a makeshift fire ring with stones the children gathered. They were all having a great time.

Suddenly a very haggard woman came around the van and said, "Are these kids bothering you?"

Campground Murders

I turned and said, "No, they're being very helpful. We're going to have a bonfire and roast marshmallows. Care to join us?"

"Oh, God, no. If you can keep them happy for a while, I'd be very happy." She turned quickly and went back around the van.

I looked at Penny. "That's what having too many children does to you. Her husband must be a rabbit."

It finally got dark, and we had the fire going. The kids were all sitting safely at a proper distance from the fire, according to Penny, sticks in hand with marshmallows on the ends.

Penny sat next to me on the picnic table smiling.

"You look happy," I said.

"This is nice. Despite the RV Park from Hell. So far these kids have been well behaved. Their mother must not be able to handle such a crowd."

"Yep, and now that we are keeping them entertained, their mother and father are probably working on child number fourteen," I said with an evil grin.

"You're so bad." She hit my arm. It'd been a while since she had done that.

Bob Moats

We toasted marshmallows, and the children were getting restless. I stood and told them we had to leave early in the morning so we wanted to go to sleep. They all moaned about having to go back to their campsite, but did leave. I was surprised.

There was still a little fire going and Penny was roasting another marshmallow. She aimed the flaming goop at me, and I said, "Keep that away from me. I have no love for them."

"You old poop," she said.

"Hey, that's from 'On Golden Pond,' the play and the movie with Jane and Henry Fonda.

"I know, I saw it a dozen times. Shall we go in the van and suck face?" she said in her best Katherine Hepburn imitation.

I put out the fire and we went into the van. The campground was quiet. I wondered why the children weren't noisier. They were probably outside the van listening to us. I peeked out the back window and could not see any one. It had me worried. Maybe the owner had grabbed the children and put them in his torture chamber under his house.

"Are you coming to bed?" Penny asked.

Campground Murders

"Yeah, I'm just wondering why it's so quiet," I said.

"Stop worrying and get in here."

I did.

The next morning there were thirteen children at our van. I opened the side door and was surprised by the crowd. "Can I do something for you?" I asked.

"Can Willy come out and play?" one boy asked.

I was trying not to laugh. Behind me Penny was laughing. She picked up Willy and pushed me out of the van. She put the dog down and said, "Now be careful, he's a small dog."

They were chasing Willy around playing tag as I was packing up the van to go. About twenty minutes later, we bid farewell to the children, and I suggested they play tag with each other. They ran off and we got into the van and drove out.

"I'm going to miss that place," Penny said.

"What? The RV Park from Hell?" I said, smiling.

"Okay, it wasn't so bad. Now we will be going straight up to Washington State into Seattle. Just follow my lead."

I didn't answer, I just listened. We drove up through California into Oregon and then into Washington. I wasn't crazy about driving twelve and a half hours, but I had this thing about a challenge. I let Penny take a nap in the back while I was on a long stretch of road. I had the CD player quietly blasting out the Fifth Dimension, a great group from the seventies. I was singing along when Penny came back up.

"Hey, Sweetie, are we close?" she asked.

"I have no idea, you're the navigator. I just stay on the road until we get there."

She sat and looked at the map, then her phone's navigation app. "Sweetie, we are on the wrong road. You're going away from Seattle. You turned the wrong way at Olympia. We're on the 101 north."

"Well, what's up here? We can explore," I said, trying to cover my mistake.

She studied the map and her navigation then said, "Well there's a small town called Brinnon straight ahead. It has a campground, too. We can stop there for the day and then swing back around to Seattle.

"Sounds like a winner to me. Is this a campground from hell?" I asked.

She laughed and said, "I hope so, the last one was nice. According to the app, this one is on the AAA recommended list of campgrounds."

"Alcoholics Anonymous? What do they have to do with Campgrounds?" I was kidding, I knew what AAA was. I even had their road service.

"Don't be a goof. You know the Auto Club. You have their road service."

She caught me. I couldn't put anything over on my wife.

*

Chapter 3

It was now around ten in the evening. It was dark but we found the campground and checked in. It was a nice place and the electric hookups were up to code. I got the van set up for the night, and Penny and I sat on the picnic table relaxing. I was beat from almost thirteen hours of driving.

"Did you see that beautiful water on the way up?" she asked.

I reached over to the map on the table and looked at it. "That water was called the Hood Canal. Strange, it's awful big for a canal. But I guess they make them big up here."

My cell phone buzzed. Penny gave me her look. I took the phone out and checked the caller ID. It was Trapper. Penny said I could answer it.

"Hey partner, what's up? You haven't burned down the office, have you?" I asked, and put the phone on speaker.

I could hear him laugh. "Nope, the building is still standing. Just wanted to see how you kids are doing."

Penny yelled softly, "He got us lost."

"I only took a different way to get to Seattle," I defended.

"Yeah, about a hundred miles out of the way," she said. "And a whole lot of water between us and Seattle.

Trapper laughed and said, "Leave it up to you, Jim. Where are you?"

Campground Murders

"Small town called Brinnon. We just got here and haven't explored yet. May take tomorrow and check it out," I said.

"Well, everything is good here. No problems. Lynn and Deacon are resting after they took the baby home. Earl, Paula and I have been over to help them get settled. They asked about you guys."

"Tell them we're fine. We'll be back in a couple weeks, in time for Penny to go national with her show. Say hi to everyone for us," I said.

"Will do. Just making sure you guys are all right and safe. I'll call in a couple days to check in," he said.

"You do that. Thanks buddy," I said, and we disconnected.

"It's nice to have friends who care," Penny said.

"Yes, it is. Now are we really out of beer?"

"I looked in the van, and the box was empty. Did you forget to pack it?"

"Seriously? You think I would forget to pack the beer. I saw a small gas station general store on the way here. Shall we take a ride?"

Bob Moats

The only bad thing about having a motorhome van, if you want to run into town, you have to take the thing out of the campground. I thought about buying a sub-compact car and towing the thing behind us to run around in, but the gas usage on the van would be a lot. Or we could get matching motor scooters. That would be cute.

We drove out of the campground and down the highway to the store. I pulled in and parked next to a nice shiny sheriff's car. Penny and I walked into the store, and we started getting stares from the people at the counter.

"Sheesh, they even know you out here?" I said. "Your last national show has been off the air for over three years. You must be hard to forget."

Penny smiled and said, "I regret that they recognize me in this getup. Camping attire is not my style."

I went straight to the beer cooler and took out a thirty pack. Penny grabbed some chips and other snacks then we went to the counter.

There was an older woman at the register, and she giggled. "Are you Penny Wickens?"

Penny smiled and said she was. The woman pulled the microphone at the counter and yelled so the whole store could hear, "Mabel, get up here. You're not going to believe this."

I stood back and let the women gather around Penny, admiring her. I looked over and saw a tall man in a sheriff's uniform moving up next to me.

He smiled and said, "We don't get many celebrities out here. Is she your wife?"

I smiled and said, "Yep, she is. And I'm not a celebrity. Well, away from Las Vegas I'm not."

"You folks from Vegas? My wife and I got married there last year."

"Yes, we're from Vegas. I have a private investigating and security firm there."

"Ah, you're a P.I.? We don't get many of those around here either. We just get FBI and crazed serial killers." He gave me a smile.

"Now you have me curious. Can you elaborate?"

"Ever hear of the NY Slasher?" he asked.

"Of course. Oh wow, that was here that he bit the dust. And that author who was copycatting him. I read about that."

Bob Moats

"Yep, I was the one who shot the bastard." He gave me a smile.

I turned to shake his hand. He took mine. The man had a nice grip. I liked him already.

"I'm Jim Richards. My wife, of course, is the famous Penny Wickens. But I'm sure you figured that out."

"Yeah, I got that. I'm Dave Chandler, Jefferson County Sheriff. What are you doing out of Vegas?"

"We're on a vacation. A much deserved vacation. Had a big case of murdered lawyers, and we caught the criminal. Well, I should say that Penny took the bad guy down. She's an amazing woman."

"I know my wife used to watch her show on the CW. Too bad it's over now."

"Well, good news. She's coming back in a couple weeks. From Las Vegas this time. So tell your wife she can watch again."

"You and your wife must live an exciting life. She gets to meet celebrities and you get to fight crime."

"I'm sure you must have your share of crime up here," I said.

Campground Murders

"Well, other than the couple serial killers and one terrorist with a deadly virus, we are a peaceful little town," he said with a smile.

"Uh, that terrorist with the virus, was that the one that was turning people into zombies?"

"Please don't bring that up. I'm still trying to live that down. We still get people coming through here looking for the zombies. They were unfortunate people who were subjected to a deadly virus that made them do bad things."

"I understand. I had my own terrorist try to unleash a virus in Vegas. We caught him on the top of the Stratosphere just as he was releasing the toxin."

"Well, now I know you. I heard about that from an FBI friend of mine, Warren Stevens. You wouldn't know him, would you?"

"Sorry the name isn't familiar. I have some friends in the FBI also. Good to have them on your side."

"Yes, it is," he said as Penny came over to us.

"Babe, this is Sheriff Dave Chandler. His wife is a fan also." I looked at the sheriff and said, "I can't take her anywhere without people spotting her."

"Good to meet you, sheriff. Now if I can tear my husband away, we need to get back to our campground," Penny said to me.

"Of course, nice to meet you, too. Maybe before you leave our town, could I impose on you to stop by our home for dinner and meet my wife? She'd be so thrilled."

"That would be real nice. I'm afraid our vacation will be a lot of restaurants and eating canned goods in the van. A nice home cooked meal would be a real treat," Penny said.

Dave handed me his card, I gave him mine. We agreed to meet in a day or so for the dinner date. I paid for the beer and snacks and we left the store.

"He seemed real nice. For a cop," Penny said.

"Being married to me, you know lots of cops. Most of them are nice. Deacon would be on the top of the list for nice cops. Followed by Trapper and Lynn."

"They all are good people. Do you think Lynn having the baby will affect her job?"

I thought on that and then said, "Hard to say. I know Lynn is dedicated to her work. But having a baby can change your life. We'll see."

We pulled back into the camping space and I hooked up the van to the electricity and the waste disposal for the toilet. We went back to the picnic table and opened our beer and chips. This was different than on our couch. Something was missing.

I laughed and said, "Shall I get out the portable TV?"

*

Chapter 4

It was after midnight and I couldn't sleep so I took Willy for a walk around the campground, admiring all the huge motorhomes and travel trailers. I liked my motorhome van. It was small enough to handle and had enough room to live in. Okay, so it wasn't very big, and it felt cramped sometimes, especially with Penny bringing just about every piece of clothing she had. I swear, she must have thought we would be out of town for a couple months.

I saw a sheriff's car at the office by the entrance, so went to see if it was Sheriff Dave Chandler. I looked in the window and saw him with a deputy, talking to the lady behind the counter. I went in, and they turned to look at me.

Bob Moats

"Hey, Jim. I see you have dog walking duties," Dave said.

I went to the counter and smiled. "Couldn't sleep. Actually, the dog is walking me."

Dave leaned down to ruffle Willy's fur. Willy tried climbing up his arm. "I think he smells my dog. I should say, my wife's dog. An Airedale Terrier. I prefer a dog this size though. Less work."

"They're all work. His name is Willy. Named after a friend of mine," I said.

He smiled and said, "Our dog is named Van Gogh, after the painter. Long story."

"Yeah, I have a long story about my dog's name, too. I think we all have long stories."

"Jim, this is one of my deputies, Virgil. Virgil, this is Jim Richards, P.I. from Las Vegas."

Virgil held his hand out, and I took it. He had a hard grip, but not crushing. I usually judge men by their handshake. He seemed to be tough and yet friendly.

"Good to meet you, Mr. Richards. Dave told me about who your wife is. I have to admit to watching her show."

Campground Murders

"I'll tell her that. She loves to hear about fans. So, is something brewing here?" I asked Dave.

"No, we're just checking the place, see if it's quiet. No trouble and a quiet night. I called my wife, and she's climbing the walls to meet your wife. She said to ask if tomorrow night is all right with you two for dinner."

"I'll check with Penny, but I'm sure it will be fine with her." It looked like we'd be there another night, I thought. That was all right. I wasn't real crazy about climbing the Space Needle.

"Good, how about seven? I'll give you the directions to our home. I think you'll like it. My wife, Sarah is her name, bought it when she first came out here from New York before we met and lived together. The house has had a few shootings of criminals in it, but we just change the blood soaked rugs and go on." He started to laugh at the thought. I liked this man's sense of humor.

Virgil asked, "Aren't you that writer of those murder novels? The ones about your adventures fighting crime?"

"Yes, I do write books. They are selling well. You read crime books?" I asked him.

"I sure do. I learn how to do my job better by reading those books," Virgil said.

"Virgil is a great deputy and a better friend. He's saved my butt a few times. And my wife's."

Virgil was turning red, and I said, "I have some paperbacks of my first couple books in my van if you'd like an autographed copy, Virgil."

"Wow, that would be great! Thanks so much," he said.

"I'll give them to Dave tomorrow night at his house."

"Great, thanks again."

"Well, I'll get my puppy back out into the night to chase fireflies. I haven't seen them in years." I went to the door and then stopped. "See you tomorrow night, Dave." Then I went out.

Willy was bouncing around chasing bugs and the occasional firefly. It was moist with the canal so close. They say it rains a lot in Seattle, but I've heard it doesn't rain that much. We made it back to our van and went in. Penny was still asleep and quietly snoring. I slipped out of my clothes and slid under the sheets. It was cool and comfy. Willy curled up between Penny and me, and I must have drifted off soon after. The country air will do that to you.

Campground Murders

The next morning Penny was in the small kitchen doing something at the stove. I could smell eggs and got up. I smiled at her and closed the thin door separating the bathroom from the kitchen after going in.

"Don't you stink up the place now," she said through the partition. I laughed and tried not to do so.

We sat on the picnic table eating her breakfast of eggs and bacon. "I wish Angelo were here to make his great breakfasts for us," Penny said.

"I'm happy with your breakfast. It's just as good."

"So when do we go entertain the sheriff and his wife?"

"Tonight at seven. His wife is anxious to meet you."

"Just when did you find this out?" she asked.

"Last night when I took Willy out for a walk. The sheriff was at the main office and we talked. Remind me to take a couple of my books for his deputy. He's a fan. He's your fan, too. Said he used to watch you. You know you have a lot of people who like you."

Bob Moats

"I'm just so loveable. That's why you married me."

"Sure, and the sex wasn't bad either." I smiled and took another bite of the bacon.

Willy came bounding out of the van on his little stairs I built for him. He came over, and Penny put down his bowl of food for him. He tore into it as I said, "This air makes you hungry, too."

"Yes, it does. And sleepy. So what are we doing today?" she asked.

"We can explore the town. I don't know how much there is to do here. I'll ask the girl in the office. We can go see the canal, too."

"Works for me. I love the water." She smiled.

"Hey, maybe you can take a swim in the canal."

"Are you kidding? That water is probably freezing. It comes in from the Pacific Ocean."

"Makes you appreciate that heated pool back home." I laughed.

"I miss it already. We need to stop in a motel so I can use their pool if they have one," she said.

Campground Murders

"I'll look for one specifically with that feature." I swallowed the last of my bacon and stood, taking my paper plate to the trash.

We finished up and gathered what we didn't want to leave lying around when we drove out to explore the town. I drove out the road to the main office and parked. "Shall we go in and see what there is to do around this place?"

Penny gathered up Willy, and we went in. The woman who was behind the counter did a double take when she saw Penny.

"My gawd, you are Penny Wickens," she said as she came to the counter. "I heard from Lois Carter that you were here. She talked to Sarah Chandler, and she confirmed it. May I have your autograph, please?"

I whispered to her, "You should have brought your photos. You could make a ton of money selling them."

She whacked my arm quickly and took the pen the woman handed her. "Make it out to Virginia, please." On a sheet of paper Penny signed the request and her name then handed it back to the woman.

"Oh, thank you so much. This is really a special day. Now, what can I do for you?"

"Well, we need to explore the town. Can you recommend places to visit?" I said.

"Well, this isn't the most adventurous place. We have a great view of the Hood Canal at the turnout north of town. There is a small beach if you feel brave enough to swim."

I looked at Penny when the woman said that. She was smiling.

She handed us a brochure of places for local interest, like an ancient spring fed wishing well and a couple historical homes where early settlers lived. There was no amusement park or even a movie theatre.

"There are movie theatres across the canal, if you don't mind a long drive. If you're hungry there's the Halfway House Restaurant."

"Thanks, but we are dining with the sheriff tonight," Penny said.

The woman looked puzzled and said, "You mean Sarah is going to actually cook?"

*

Chapter 5

"I wonder what she meant by that?" Penny asked me as we went back to the van.

"I'm presuming that this Sarah, the sheriff's wife, isn't a great cook. Sound familiar?" I said.

"You better not be referring to me, or you're dead meat," she growled.

"No, dear, not you. I wouldn't presume to speak for your culinary abilities."

We drove around the town sight-seeing. There wasn't much to see, but it was a quaint little place. We visited a few landmarks and went by the water processing plant. Okay, that wasn't great, but we heard it was the place where a terrorist was going to dump his virus.

We drove back to our camping space and parked. "I need to take a quick nap. You interested?" I asked.

"Not with you. You snore worse during a nap," she responded.

Bob Moats

I got out of the van, pulled a chaise-lounge out of the back storage and opened it next to the van. I lay down on it and said, "Wake me when it's time to get ready to go for our last meal."

"I'll tell Sarah you said that," she said and hooked Willy up to his leash. "I'm taking a walk before you start scaring the little animal with your log sawing." She walked away, and I put my head back down and hoped for a little nap.

I was dreaming of hanging off the Space needle, looking down to the pavement below, when I was shaken awake. "Wake up, Sweetie. Time to get ready."

I opened one eye and saw her smiling at me. "Is it time to drive home?" I asked.

"Get up! You arranged this dinner. Now suffer with it," she said and went into the van. I pulled myself up from the lounger very slowly. My back was feeling terrible from napping on my back. I didn't like being on my back. It hurt after a while, but it was not easy to sleep sideways on a lounger.

I did manage to get up and go into the van to the back bedroom. Penny had clothes set out for me on the bed. "Want to dress me, too?" I asked.

Campground Murders

"No, get dressed on your own," she said and went to the bathroom.

I changed and put on the clothes she had out. Actually she had better taste than I did, so it was a good choice. I admired myself in the full length mirror on the bathroom door and went out. Penny was gathering things to put in the van. I helped. We were packed and ready to go, even though we had about forty minutes to be there. I studied the map that Dave had given me. The house was north of town on the Canal. We drove out slowly, through town and to the house.

It was interesting. I figured it was an octagonal design. I had seen them before. This one had walls of glass that gave a great view of the property and the canal behind it. I parked and we got out. Penny carried Willy until we saw what reaction their dog gave him.

Airedale Terriers are large and probably could gulp Willy in one bite. We went up to the porch, and the door opened before I could knock. It was Dave.

"Welcome, Jim, Penny. Come on in," he said as a large dog came bouncing out and jumped up on me.

"Van Gogh, get down now and get back in here!" came a voice from behind Dave. The dog flinched and ran back in the house. A smallish, trim woman came around Dave and smiled at Penny.

Bob Moats

"Mrs. Wickens, so good to meet you." She beamed.

"Actually, it's Mrs. Richards now. Wickens is my stage name since I got married to Jim. Call me Penny, please."

"Well, Penny, please call me Sarah. Welcome to our home. Come on in." We went into the vestibule as Sarah noticed Willy. "Oh my God, what a cute dog. I'm sure you can put him down, Van Gogh won't hurt him."

I was sure Penny was concerned for her dog. She looked at Van Gogh peeking from behind Sarah and slowly held Willy down to the floor. Van Gogh came over and, after sniffing him, gave Willy a big lick with his tongue. Willy barked and Van Gogh backed up a little. We all laughed.

"I think they'll get along," Penny said and put Willy on the floor. As soon as Willy was free, he went after the big dog who turned and ran out of the vestibule.

"Big brave dog," Dave said, with a laugh. "They'll be alright. Come on in." We went into a very nice living room. Huge, airy and the windows went from the floor to the ceiling. The view of the water with the sun shining as it was going down was spectacular.

Campground Murders

"Beautiful home you have," Penny said to Sarah. I could see Sarah was celebrity struck.

"Thank you so much. I used to watch you every day when I would edit and write my books." She suddenly realized something. "Jim, you're an author of a great series of books. It's so good to meet you, too."

"Well, I have to confess, after I met Dave and found out you guys were involved in the NY Slasher case, I looked you up on Google. You're an author, too."

She smiled and turned a little red. "Yes, I am. But not as good as you. Please sit. Would you like something to drink?"

"If you have a beer, that would be fine," I said. I looked at Dave. "I'm not driving, and Penny is my designated driver."

Dave laughed and said, "You both can drink. I'll be sure there are no cops to stop you."

Dave brought us our drinks as we sat in the living room. Van Gogh was trying to give a tennis ball to Willy. The ball was almost as big as the little dog. They were running around the room with the ball, playing.

"I'm glad to see they are getting along," I said.

Sarah said, "Van Gogh doesn't have any other dogs to play with. Well, we have one friend with a dog, but it's not very friendly with Van Gogh." She turned to Penny. "Now I want to know about this new show you are doing. Is it going to be like your old show?"

Penny laughed and said, "It's basically the same, but from Las Vegas this time. More celebrities and more fun. You should come out sometime and I'll give you a good seat to watch from and a tour around Vegas."

Sarah looked at Dave. "We got married in Vegas. I really loved the city while we were there."

"Jim and I got married in Vegas also, before we moved there," Penny replied.

"Do you like it there?" Dave asked.

"Love it. Jim lived there before we moved there. He couldn't get the city out of his system," Penny said.

"Do they have many jobs for sheriffs?" Dave asked.

"I personally know most of the police in Vegas. If you are interested, I could get you an interview.

Campground Murders

From what I've read about your abilities to take down serial killers and terrorists, I'm sure they'd hire you," I said.

"It's something to think about," Dave said. He smiled at Sarah and said, "Feel like moving there?"

"Dave, I know you grew up here, but I'm starting to miss big city life." She looked at us and said, "I grew up in New York City. It's a cultural shock to live here in the country. I think Las Vegas would be a cultural shock, too. But a good one."

"Something to talk about, honey," Dave said. "How's the dinner doing?" he asked her.

She suddenly gave a shocked look, stood and said, "Excuse me." She rushed out of the room.

Penny stood and said, "I'll see if she needs help." She went out, too.

"Is your wife as good a cook as mine?" I asked.

"I can't say. How's your wife's cooking?"

I looked over to the doorway and quietly said, "I prefer to eat out."

"Then they are the same," he said with a laugh.

A half hour later Penny and Sarah were busy working in the kitchen getting the dinner ready. I told Dave, "Maybe the two of them together will turn out something good." He agreed.

We were all sitting around the table eating the roast, potatoes and veggies when the phone rang.

"If that's a telemarketer, I'll hunt them down. Excuse me," Dave said and stood. He went to the vestibule to the phone on the table out there and answered. He listened, said a couple things and then hung up. He stood thinking.

Penny leaned toward me and said quietly, "Why do I feel like there was a murder?"

*

Chapter 6

Dave came back into the dining room and stood behind his chair. "Uh...that was my other deputy, Mike. He said there's a small problem in town that needs my attention. Jim, would you like to ride along while the ladies sit and talk?"

Penny whispered to me, "Yep. It's a murder. You did this, you know."

Campground Murders

I looked at her and said, "Stop that." I turned my attention back to Dave and said, "Sure, I'd like that."

"Good, now you can see how a small town sheriff works. Shall we go?" Dave said.

I stood and kissed Penny then followed Dave out to his car. Sarah came to the door and yelled, "Don't you two end up in some bar."

I could hear Dave laugh to himself. I got in the passenger side and buckled up. "I see your wife has a sarcastic sense of humor like mine," I said.

"Yes, she does. Now this little emergency that called me away, well, it seems there was a murder at your campground."

That sent a chill through me. Of course Penny would have her ammunition to blame me for it. I didn't want to tell Dave about my curse, so I just rode along without mentioning that.

"Did you get any details?" I asked as we sped down the road, back towards the campground, with flashers and siren going.

"Mike isn't one for details. He likes to say there's a murder and leaves it up to my imagination. If it were Virgil, he would have all kinds of details, including a conspiracy of aliens attacking." Dave laughed. "I remember when we had the terrorist spreading the virus. Virgil was convinced there were zombies attacking our town. He's a good friend and a good deputy, but he loves drama."

"I have a good friend like that, too. His name is Buck and he dramatizes all my cases. When we went out to Area 51 in Nevada to investigate a murder, he believed that aliens were behind it. Of course, he was wrong, but it was fun to listen to him."

"Like a little kid, huh?" Dave asked.

"As a matter of fact, yes," I said with a smile.

We arrived at the campground where we found Dave's other deputy. Dave got out of his car and pulled out a belt from the back seat with holster and a very big Colt revolver. I had my Glock under my coat, which I probably should have told him I had.

I stopped him before we went to the crime scene and said, "Dave, I should tell you I have a weapon. It's a Glock and it is registered, but I don't know how you feel about me wearing it."

He turned and said, "Are you going to shoot me or my deputies?"

"Not today," I said with a smile.

Campground Murders

"Good. I figured you had one under your coat. It did bulge out."

"I'll talk to my tailor about that."

We got to the crime scene. It was taped off as a young man in uniform came to us.

"Jim, this is Mike, my deputy. Mike. this is Jim. He's a P.I. from out of Vegas."

"Well, we could use a good private investigator here. I'll show you where the body is."

He led us to some bushes behind a tent. "There was a man, he's over there," Mike said pointing, "His dog got loose and he followed the mutt into the bushes and found the body."

Dave bent down to the body of a man spread out in a strange fashion. Almost like a ritual killing. He was spread out with his arms and legs pointing away from his body. It reminded me of the DaVinci drawing of a man in a circle.

"Have you got an ID on him?" Dave asked Mike.

"Not yet. I didn't want to disturb the body until Doc Mitchell came to examine him."

Dave looked at me and said, "Doc Mark Mitchell is our county coroner. He survived the zombie attacks and actually stayed here to be our permanent coroner." Dave stepped back from the body and asked me, "What do you think?"

I was surprised he asked me and asked him, "How was he killed?"

Dave turned to Mike and said, "Well, how was he killed?"

"That much I did find out. He was stabbed through the heart with this." He held up a plastic bag with a knife.

"Where did you get that?" Dave asked.

"Next to the body. It's got blood on it and the victim has a gaping chest wound. So I figured it was the murder weapon."

"Very good deductive reasoning," Dave said, with a smile.

"Do you have a CSI out here?" I asked.

"Nope, we get the State Police forensic team to check our crime scenes. Mike, did you call them?" he asked.

"As soon as I was called by the campground manager. They said they'd be here in an hour."

Campground Murders

"Okay, secure the area and we'll wait." He turned and went back to the tent, looking around with his flashlight.

I always carried a pocket flashlight with really bright LEDs in it. I pulled mine out and asked, "Should we be walking around in the possible crime scene?"

"I like to do my own investigation before the State boys take over. They get a little carried away sometimes and mess up a crime scene," he said, looking into the tent. "I know your big city CSIs like to take the lead on evidence. Our forensic people aren't as sophisticated as your CSI. They tend to miss a lot. So I usually conduct my own investigation of the crime scene." He handed me gloves to put on after he put his on.

He disappeared into the tent. I stood at the opening watching him go through the personal stuff inside. He found a small leather case that looked like the same as I use to carry memory cards. He held it out to me. "Do you know what this is?" I told him. "Yep, that's right, I was just testing you," he said with a grin. He opened it and found it was empty.

"There should be memory cards in here, wouldn't you say?" he asked.

"Normally if a person has one of these it's for carrying memory cards, yes."

"So I think he had cards or was going to put cards in." Dave found a notebook and looked through it. "Lots of strange formulas in here. Do you know anything about physics?"

"I flunked math let alone physics. Sorry. Is the thing full of physics formulas or chemistry?"

"Good question. Take a look and see if you can decipher it." He handed the book to me and I went through it. The scribbles were definitely chemical formulas. I told Dave.

"Crap. I hope we don't have another terrorist plotting in my back yard," he said.

I handed the book back to him. He pulled out another leather folder, bigger this time. It looked like a personal diary. Dave opened it and thumbed through the pages. He got to the end and handed it to me. "What do you think?"

I thumbed through the pages and found photos pasted in the book. It was a small photo album. There were pages of pictures of the dead man, I presumed, and a family. A wife and two children. I felt sorry for them. They looked so happy.

Dave was still going through the belongings when he came up with a weapon. A Smith and

Campground Murders

Wesson .38 in good condition. "Now why would he need a gun?" Dave asked me.

"Usually for protection, or to murder someone," I replied.

"I hope he wasn't here to murder someone." Dave turned over the bedding and air mattress and found nothing. "Whoever killed him didn't search this tent. It was too neat when we came in."

We left the tent and Dave put the gun and books in a large plastic bag. He called Mike and told him to put them in his car. Mike went off and we stood waiting as a large black car pulled up.

"That would be Doc Mitchell. It's his death wagon as I call it." Dave laughed.

A fairly young man got out and came to us. "Hey, Doc, this is Jim Richards, famous P.I. from Las Vegas. He's consulting on this murder."

"Good to meet you, Jim," the doc said.

I was both surprised and honored that Dave included me as a consultant. Now I had helped two different police departments.

*

Chapter 7

"He was definitely stabbed through the heart, that's the cause of death. It was a good thrust, it broke the ribs. I'd say it was a man. He'd have the strength to do that," Doc Mitchell said as he examined the body.

"That sounds sexist. I'm telling Lois Carter you said that," Dave said.

"Oh damn, don't tell her. It will be all over town by tomorrow," he said with a laugh.

Dave turned to me and said, "Lois Carter is our local gossip. She was the one who introduced me to Sarah." He looked back at Doc and asked, "How long has he been dead?"

"Well, the temp out here is normal and his internal body temp hasn't dropped very far. I'd say about two hours. Give or take fifteen minutes." He smiled.

Dave turned to Mike and said, "Go around the area and ask the campers if they saw what happened or any suspicious persons walking around."

Campground Murders

Mike hesitated.

"What's the matter?" Dave asked.

"I hate talking to strangers, they scare me," he said.

"Mike you're a deputy, a law enforcement officer. You have to talk to strangers. You talk to strangers when you give out speeding tickets, and you enjoy that."

"Yeah...I guess I do. But these people are here camping with their families and I'm talking to them about murder."

Dave thought a moment. "Yeah, I guess you need to be diplomatic and not frighten anyone. We don't need to empty out the campground. Now go find out what you can."

"Okay, but I'm under protest." Mike went off into the dark and to the next campsite.

Dave turned to me and said, "Mike can be a little stubborn at times, and a little lazy. But he's a good cop when he works."

A large van pulled up to where we were and three men got out. Dave said, "It's the State Police forensics. Hopefully they can find something besides what I found. Even in the dark."

One of the men pulled out a couple light trees and set them up while another man came over to us.

"Hey, Sheriff. Long time no see. Did you murder someone just to get us out here again?" he asked.

Dave laughed and said, "No, I don't need any more excitement, Steve. I've had enough to last a while."

"Think this could be another serial killer, like Frank Draegon?" he asked.

"I hope not. Or a copycat. I'm hoping it was a lover's spat. I'll let you go to work. Thanks for coming out so late."

"It's our job, and it's overtime," he said with a big laugh.

Dave and I went out to the street and stood watching the techs light up the scene. They plugged the lights into the power boxes on the site and the area went bright. They started to examine every inch of ground and in the tent.

"I should tell Steve that I raided the tent. Be right back." Dave went to the man named Steve and talked to him. I stood looking down the street and could see

Campground Murders

Mike under a street lamp talking to a young couple. They were very animated, arms waving around and saying something loudly. Not loud enough for me to understand them, but I could hear them talking. Mike kept looking back to the site I was standing at.

Dave came back to me. "Steve figured I wouldn't wait for them. He said to turn in the evidence later."

I pointed to Mike and the couple and said, "Seems your deputy found some talkative witnesses."

Dave looked down to them as Mike said something and came back to us. We waited for him to amble up the road. When he got near us, he said, "There's a newlywed couple down there who said they were interrupted by two men running around their campsite. The one man was trying to get away from the other and then they both ran away."

"Did they get a good look at the men?" I asked.

Mike looked at me and said, "It was dark, they didn't want anyone seeing what they were doing. Newlyweds as I said."

"I get the image, Mike," Dave said with a laugh.

"But the man said he got a quick look at the pursuer when he shined a flashlight at them. He may be able to identify him."

"Good, we need to see if we can get Walt to come out to do a sketch." Dave turned to me and said, "Walt is with the FBI in Seattle. He and another agent are friends and helped us with both our serial killers and the terrorist. Walt is a genius with computers, and he has one of those programs that assemble a sketch of the suspect."

"We have the same in Vegas PD. It's an amazing program," I said. "Are you calling the FBI in on this?"

"No, just having the sketch done by Walt on an unofficial request. Of course I'd like to have my friend Warren Stevens join us in our investigation if he's free."

"You're like me. I go on a case but I have a couple police detectives that I like to work with. They usually solve the case and I enjoy the help," I said.

"Nice to have friends in the right places."

"Yep," I replied.

"Well, I hope we aren't here all night. Sarah will have your wife in pajamas and having a pajama party." Dave laughed.

Campground Murders

"I'm sure Penny would be happy with that if the wine is good and they have a lot to talk about," I said.

"Sarah can talk her arm off if Penny lets her."

Mike came to us from the crime scene. "They haven't found much. A couple footprints in the dirt that they're taking plaster casts of. The vic has been established by Doc Mitchell as Kenneth Laymen from Tacoma. Now why would he be camping here in Brinnon? They have far better campgrounds around Tacoma."

"How did Doc figure the ID?"

"The vic had a wallet in his cargo pants, in the bottom pocket. I'll run the name at the station and see what comes up," Mike said.

"Good, Mike, do that. Let me know what you find," Dave said and the deputy went to his car and drove off.

"Do you only have the two deputies?" I asked.

"Mike and Virgil, yes. That's all I can afford with our budget. I'd like to have more, but even with all the crime we've had I can't get another deputy."

"How about getting a police auxiliary going? No pay, but men willing to be interns."

"I like your thinking. I'll take it to the town council and see if they have a problem with it. They probably will worry about liabilities, like someone getting killed. But it's worth a try. At least having a few people who will man the station when we are out on the road will be a great help."

We stood doing nothing but talking about our past cases. Just bragging on our accomplishments. About an hour later Steve came to us and said, "We're done for now. We got a few bits of trace and the knife you'll provide will help." He smiled.

"I'll get you what I found," Dave said and went to his car.

"You're Jim Richards, aren't you?" Steve asked.

"Yes, I am. Surprised you know me," I replied.

"I go to Vegas a lot. I've seen you on the TV news there. You're some hero, aren't you?"

"I speak in all modesty, but yes, I'm a hero." I laughed aloud and shook his hand.

"Good to meet you finally. I can't seem to stay away from news about crime wherever I'm at. Most of my traveling buddies think I'm nuts watching the news late at night when I should be losing my money to the casinos."

"Save your money, the house takes it all. One person out of a thousand will hit a good win and take home money. If they don't lose it again gambling."

"I'm not much of a gambler, but I do like to visit the strip clubs."

"Ah, I have a friend who would like to meet you. He's a fan of strippers and hookers."

"Give me your card and the next time I'm in Vegas, I look him up."

I handed him my card with the office number and laughed. "Just ask for Trapper and say I sent you."

*

Chapter 8

Dave's cell phone rang and he answered, "Yeah, Mike. Whatcha got?" He listened, pulled a note pad from his pocket and wrote something. He finished the call and said to me, "This Laymen guy was reported missing by his wife. Mike is going to see if he can track her down in Tacoma by phone. I may have to go visit her tomorrow, if need be."

"A missing man pops up murdered in a campground miles from home. He has a gun, a book of chemical formulas and is followed by a killer. I think this would make a good book," I said.

Dave laughed. "Do you write about all your adventures in Vegas?"

"There and when I lived in Michigan. I started my firm there and move to Vegas about four years ago," I replied. "I wrote about the first couple murders then it got to be fun to write. I just started my fourteenth book."

"Well, Sarah only has the two, but it keeps her happy."

"I'll have to give her book a read through. Is your sketch artist coming out tonight?"

"Walt? No, in the morning. Mike called him and he said he'd start first thing. I should go tell the newlyweds to hang around. Care to join me in interrupting them?"

"Maybe they're in for the night," I said.

"I'm rude that way," he said with a laugh.

We walked down to the campsite where Mike found the young couple. We went to the tent and

Campground Murders

Dave called to them. There was no answer. Dave tried again, same result. He went to the tent and carefully peeked in. He turned to me and said, "It's empty."

"Maybe they took a walk," I said.

"Possible. We'll wait for a little while. Doc still hasn't taken the body out. We may need to help him." We went back to the crime scene as Doc was backing his vehicle into the site. He got out, opened the back of the wagon and then went to the body. He had put it in the body bag. We went to him and helped put the body in the wagon.

"Thanks, guys. I'll have more for you tomorrow after I examine him." He got in his car and drove off.

Dave and I were alone then at the crime scene. "I'm never comfortable around crime scenes. I had enough of them when I was on the PD in Tacoma. I was in homicide."

"Really? I'll have to talk to my friends in LVPD homicide and see if they can get you a job," I said.

Dave laughed and said, "I like being a country sheriff. It's quiet and easy going. The worst we get during the week is speeders through town. Okay, we've had our share of serial killers and terrorists, but I prefer the quiet."

"If you ever change your mind, let me know," I said.

"Shall we go back and see what our wives are up to?"

"I'm afraid to find out," I said with a smile.

"First, I want to check on the young couple." He went out, I followed and we walked to the site again. It was still vacant.

"This is starting to worry me. If the killer knows they can identify him, they may be in danger." Dave pulled his cell phone out and made a call. "Mike, come back to the campground and see if you can find the newlyweds. They seem to be missing." He listened and then hung up. "We'll wait until he gets here."

About five minutes later, Mike showed up. Dave gave him instructions for finding the couple, said he'd be home and to call if he found them. We went to his car and drove out.

Driving back I asked, "Are you happy with Sarah? I'm sorry if that's personal. I'm just curious."

He laughed and said, "Of course I am. She's the best thing to happen to me even after moving back here from Tacoma. Out there I was living with this hot number who drove me nuts. We finally cooled down to the point of breaking up, and I wasn't going to get involved again. Then Lois pushed me and Sarah together. Sarah had come out here from New York to get away from the memory of her husband's murder. She really loved him, and it was hard for her to start over. We went slow at first, then it got serious. I was there for her, as a friend and eventually a lover." He went quiet. I wasn't going to break his concentration.

Finally I said, "I knew Penny from high school. I had a small crush on her and didn't know until forty years later that she had a crush on me. All those years wasted. But we are making up for it now. She's the best thing to happen to me, too."

We drove on and got to the house shortly after talking more about our wives. Dave pulled into the drive. There were three cars in front of us. "What the hell," Dave said. He pulled around the cars and parked on the lawn in front of the house.

We exited the car and went up to the porch. Dave peeked in the side windows around the door and laughed. "This is not what I expected," he said as he opened the door. We went through the vestibule and into the living room. There we found six women along with Penny and Sarah. Sarah jumped up and came to us.

"I couldn't help it. I called Lois and told her who was here. She called a few friends and they stopped by. I hope you don't mind, Jim?"

"I have no problems with it." I looked at Penny who was grinning from ear to ear. "If Penny is fine with it."

Penny came over and said, "These women are hilarious. They tell the best stories about their lives." She got close to me and said, "We may be here a couple days more. Lois is throwing a party for me at the VFW hall."

I was trying not to laugh. She smelled like she had enough to drink. "Okay, fine with me. I'm helping Dave with his case."

"Ah yes, it was murder, wasn't it? Who was it?"

"I'll tell you tomorrow. You have people waiting for you," I said pointing to the six women, all starstruck.

"Oh, yes. You and Dave go talk as I entertain my fans." She turned and went back to the women.

Dave came over to me and said to follow him. He went to the kitchen and took four beers out of the fridge, then went to a door in the back of a laundry room. We ended up sitting on wooden deck chairs facing the canal.

Campground Murders

"You have a very beautiful back yard," I said.

"I like it. It's especially beautiful in the morning as the sun comes up. Now tell me about how you stopped the crazy man with the virus."

We talked until Sarah and Penny came out, six beers each later.

"Are you boys beating your chests about your adventures?" Sarah asked.

Penny was weaving a little, and she looked sleepy. I stood and went to her, putting my arm around her. "Hi, Sweetie. Having fun yet?" she said, her words a little slurred.

"Not as much as you are. Shall we go back to the campground?" I asked her.

Dave stood and came over. "Since you have your house with you, why not just camp out in the front yard? I can hook you up to the electricity. That way you don't have to drive back."

Penny perked up and said to Sarah, "You don't mind?"

"Hell, no. We can stay up all night and talk," Sarah said, sounding just as tired as Penny. Or as drunk.

Bob Moats

I said to Dave, "If you don't mind, I'll take you up on that offer. I don't feel like going back to the…" I didn't want to say crime scene… "campground this late."

"Great. Let the girls go back in the house and we'll get you set up out front." Penny and Sarah went back in and Dave and I went out to the front. Dave pulled an extension cord from a shed and hooked it to an outside plug. We plugged it into the van, and there was power. I took him inside the van and he marveled at the way it was laid out.

"I love this. It has all the comforts of home. You could live in here."

"If Penny ever throws me out, I will," I said with a laugh.

*

Chapter 9

The four of us were in the living room talking when the phone rang again. Penny gave me a bleary eye as Dave got up to answer.

He listened, then finished and hung up. He stood in the vestibule thinking.

Sarah said, "I'm used to the calls in the night." She looked at the clock on the wall. "Even at midnight, he gets calls. Usually for some drunks at the VFW hall. Mike can't handle the drunks himself so he calls Dave."

Penny was nodding off. I let her put her head on my shoulder with my arm around her. I said to Sarah, "Penny isn't much of a drinker. You'll have to forgive her. I can drink a good number of beers, and I'm just happy. Give Penny a few glasses of wine and it's good-night, world."

Sarah laughed. "Don't worry about it. I come from an Italian family and we've drunk wine every day for years so it doesn't bother me."

Dave came back and said, "We have a new problem. You can just relax, but I have to go."

Bob Moats

I moved Penny off my side and let her lie on the couch. "If you don't mind, I'd like to go with you. I'll take Penny out to the van."

"Jim, let her just rest there. I'll watch her until you guys get back," Sarah said.

"Thanks, Sarah," I said and stood. I looked at Penny smiling while she slept with her head on the couch pillow. "She'll be out for a while." I looked at Dave and said, "Shall we go?"

Dave went to the door followed by me. In the car I said, "I hope the newlyweds aren't dead."

"No, but they found the girl unconscious, and her husband is missing. This is not good. I don't want trouble to start." Dave hit the siren and flashers as we traveled back to the campground. We arrived and found an ambulance just loading the girl.

Mike waved to us as we pulled around the road to where they were at. We exited the car and went to Mike.

"What's the deal?" Dave asked.

"I was wandering around trying to find the couple when some woman came running up to me and said she found a girl in the bushes next to her tent. That's the woman who found her," Mike said pointing to a rather upset woman. Dave went to her. I followed.

"Ma'am, I'm Sheriff Chandler. Can you tell me how you found her?"

"I was out getting some air and went around the camp site when I saw an arm sticking out of the brush. I went there and saw a body attached to the arm. I got my cell phone out and called 911. I was told to wait for someone to come and not to touch anything. I did see if she was alive, and she was. Poor girl."

"Did you see anyone else around the area?" Dave asked.

"No, just her and the deputy. It's late and everyone is sleeping."

"She had a new husband. He's missing now," Dave said.

"Oh dear, that's not good. Poor girl," she said again.

"Well, thank you. You may have saved her life. I'll talk to you more in the morning." He came back to me as I stood away from them.

"You have 911 out here?" I asked.

Bob Moats

"No, it goes to the main Jefferson County Sheriff's office, and they call us out here if it's from our area. I'm calling in Virgil to help find the man. I'll call a few others who help when we have a missing child in the woods. Be right back."

He went to his car and got on the radio. I was watching the ambulance medics finish strapping the woman in the vehicle. Then they drove out. Mike came to me. I asked, "Where are they taking her?"

"That's the EMS from our firehouse. They'll take her to a clinic we have here. The doctor has been called in already so he'll meet them there. Hopefully she'll be all right. She seemed very nice when I talked to them earlier."

Dave came back. "Virgil is going to gather the men to help search the area," he said. Then to me, "We've searched in the dark before for missing children. Hopefully we'll find the husband."

About a half hour later there were fifteen men and Virgil assembled in the middle of the campground as Dave gave them the rundown.

"The killer may still be on the grounds, so be careful and, for you who are packing heat, don't shoot first. This is a young guy and just married so we want to find him alive if possible. Now spread out and check the bushes carefully. Go to it."

71

Campground Murders

The men all went off in different directions as Dave was talking to Virgil. I went to them and listened.

"Virg, get hold of Warren and fill him in on this. It's probably a kidnapping now, and the FBI handles that."

Dave turned away from the deputy and said to me, "I hope this goes well."

We stood silently watching the men we could still see, checking around the area. About forty minutes later, most of the men were back. One came to Dave.

"Sorry, Dave, couldn't find him. It's getting late now, but we can look again in the morning."

"Thanks, Clarence. See you in the morning," Dave said then told the men who came in to go home and try again in the morning. By one-thirty everyone was gone. Dave looked upset. "Damn, I should have had Mike watch them when we knew they saw the man."

"Don't beat yourself up over it. Can't cover all bases. This may still work out," I said.

"I hope so. Hate to have them start out a marriage this way. I'll call the clinic and see how she's doing. Shall we go back to the house?"

"Fine with me. Even in Vegas we hardly ever work so late." I laughed.

We arrived back at the house and Penny was up having coffee with Sarah. "Well, you boys have been busy," Penny said.

"Just a little blip," I said.

"Blip, hell. Murder, I hear," Penny said.

"How did you find out so soon?" I asked.

"Just now, you gave it away."

"Oh, even drunk, you are so clever," I said.

"And you are so gullible," she said and kissed me on the cheek.

She turned to Dave and said, "Jim has this curse. Everywhere we go there's a murder. Even a thousand miles out in the ocean, we had two murders." She looked at me. "Now you should arrest him for contributing to murder," she said with a big smile.

"I'm sure he didn't have anything to do with this murder. But I may hold him in protective custody for his own good."

Campground Murders

"I don't need to be picked on. See Dave, I married a viscous, evil woman."

Dave laughed and said, "I think it's time to hit the sheets. Are you two going to be all right outside?"

"We've camped out in many different places but never before out front on the lawn of a sheriff. We'll be fine. Shall we go, babe?"

"I'm ready. This coffee isn't helping to wake me up." She stood, we said our good nights and I followed her out to the van.

Once in, I locked up the doors and set Willy down on the floor. He had been asleep in the house next to Van Gogh. It was cute, the big and small of them. He ran off to the bedroom and climbed his little stairs to the bed. He circled and plopped down. One big huff and he was out again. I hoped I could sleep that fast. I undressed while Penny was in the bathroom. I slid under the sheets and Penny came out to the bed and climbed in. She had undressed in the bathroom.

She picked up Willy and put him behind her then snuggled up to me. "Hey, big boy, are you new around here?"

I just stared at her in the semi-dark of the room, the only light coming from the bathroom. I always insisted on the light being on in case I needed to go in the middle of the night.

"Are you feeling frisky?" I said.

"Me, frisky? What gave you that idea?"

"Could be because of where you have your hands." I smiled.

*

Chapter 10

It was a good night. Penny was limber and feeling no pain. We finished our romp and then slept. It was already after two, and I had planned on getting up early. We both slept well and woke around seven. I looked out the window and saw that Dave was letting Van Gogh run for his morning dump. I went to the door of the van and said good morning.

"Did you two sleep well?" he asked.

"Uh, yeah, we did. Did you call the clinic? How's the girl?"

Campground Murders

"She's doing well. I'm going to talk to her this morning if you'd like to ride along," Dave said.

"Of course he'll ride along," came a voice from behind me. It was Penny. "I have a date with your wife to go shopping, so you two can go play cops and robbers."

"Cops and murderers," I corrected.

"Okay, just don't get yourselves killed." She gave me a kiss then went past me with Willy to the front door where Sarah was standing. They went inside.

I came away from the van and went to Dave on the porch. "Think the wife will be able to help us?"

"I hope so. I put Mike on her room, to protect her in case the killer comes back. I'll be able to see if she saw the killer, too. I talked to Walt, and he left with my friend Warren about a half hour ago. They'll be here by nine. Shall we start?"

"If the women are happy without us, I'm ready," I said.

"Sarah learned a while back, my job comes first. She amuses herself when I'm gone. Now with Penny along, I'm sure they will be gone most of the day."

Bob Moats

"I just hope Penny doesn't buy out the town. We have only so much room in the van."

A sheriff's car pulled into the drive and parked. Virgil got out and came to us. "I got everyone together at the campground, and we did a search again this morning. They found nothing. If the killer is dragging the husband around, he's most likely still in the area."

"Virgil, you are a regular Sherlock Holmes," Dave said. "Have a few men at the roads out of town checking cars. Deputize them if you have to so they can stop cars."

"Will do, Dave. Are you going to talk to the wife?"

"Yep, hopefully she knows something."

Virgil looked at me. "Got any thoughts on this?"

"I'm just observing. If I think of anything you haven't covered, I'll share," I said.

"Anything will help," Dave said.

Mike said he was going to go set up road blocks, and he left.

"Let's go talk to the wife," he said, and we went to his car.

Campground Murders

On the way over, I said, "I wonder why the killer would take the man with him. If he was finished after killing Laymen, then he would be heading out of town. I would think the body of the husband would have turned up already. Unless the killer is taking the man with him."

"I wondered the same. This isn't over, I'm afraid."

The clinic wasn't real big in size but it was adequate. We went in and Dave greeted the woman at the reception counter.

"Hey, Mary. How are you today?" he asked.

The woman beamed and said, "Very good. I heard you had a celebrity at your house."

"That's true. Penny Wickens, from the TV. This is her husband, Jim Richards." He pointed to me. I waved to her.

"Good to meet you. Is Mrs. Wickens still in town?"

"She better be or I'm stranded here," I joked.

"Of course, how dumb of me. Are you two here to see the woman who came in last night?"

"Yes, is she awake?"

"Last I knew she was resting. Her injuries were not life threatening. A blow to the head left her unconscious but alive."

"Where do we find her?"

"Second room on the left," she said.

"Is Doctor Morgan with her?"

"No, he checked in on her about ten minutes ago. Now he's checking young Bobby Wells for chicken pox."

"Ouch, that's not good. Thanks, Mary," Dave said.

"Nice to meet you, Mary," I said.

"Good to meet you, Mr. Richards."

Dave thanked her again, and we went down the hall to the room she told us. Mike was sitting on a chair and stood as we came up.

"All's quiet, Dave," Mike said.

"Thanks, Mike," he said. We entered and found the woman eating breakfast. She gave us an anxious look as we came to her.

Campground Murders

"Have you found my husband yet?" she asked.

"We're still searching. Is there anything you can remember that may help us?"

She pushed the food tray away and was thinking. "All I remember was that we were walking down the road getting some air when this person came up behind us. I looked back, and he hit me with something. I was out from there. That's all I can tell you. I'm sorry."

"Did you get a look at the man's face?" Dave asked.

"It was quick. I just got a glimpse of him. I don't know if I can give you the description."

"I have an expert FBI agent coming in to help you remember and get a sketch of the man. Now relax, he's good at what he does."

Dave's cell phone rang, and he excused himself. He answered and smiled. "You guys must have flown. We're at the clinic where Killian had his surgery. Do you remember?" He listened and said, "Good, see you shortly."

He came back to me. "That was my friend Warren. They're just coming in now. I'm sure

Warren was driving. He can turn a two hour ride into one hour."

"Killian? Is that the terrorist who had the virus?"

"Yeah, he was. He's not going to terrorize anyone now. Walt shot and killed him. I'm not for killing anyone, but some people deserve it."

"Why, Dave, are you condoning vigilantes?"

"Hell, yes. If it takes these scums off the streets, I don't care who pulls the trigger. Besides Walt is FBI, so he's allowed to shoot bad guys." He smiled at me and we went out to wait for Walt and Warren.

About five minutes later a huge black van roared into the parking lot. It screeched to a stop just before the sidewalk, and a tall man got out of the driver's side. A smaller man, looking like what a geek should look like, exited the passenger side. He looked a little pale.

"Warren, you're going to give Walt a heart attack the way you drive," Dave said to the tall man.

"He's getting used to my driving. Especially in the Dodge Charger. There are fingernail marks on the passenger side dashboard." He laughed.

Walt shifted his glasses up his nose and said, "You are a maniac behind the wheel."

Campground Murders

"Guys, this is the famous Jim Richards from Las Vegas," Dave said, pulling me over.

"Well, you aren't exactly like I imagined you. I thought you'd have a cape and red tights," Warren said, shaking my hand. "I had to read up on the virus threat that you and your partner, Buck, stopped from killing Vegas."

"Actually it turned out to be talcum powder in the container. The virus is now buried in the Vegas Valley desert somewhere. The government isn't happy they can't find it." I looked at Dave and said, "It was a small town sheriff that switched the virus with the talcum to fool the terrorist."

Warren laughed and said, "Let's hear it for small town sheriffs."

"Enough of this foolishness," Dave said. "We have a situation now. Walt did you bring your sketch program with you?"

"Of course, I never leave home without it," he said and went to the van. He slid open the side door and pulled out a small laptop.

Dave said to me, "This van is an electronic nightmare. Walt has gadgets in there that can see a woman sun bathing in New York."

Bob Moats

Walt looked back and said, "I do not." He smiled. "That equipment is back in my office."

Dave took all of us back into the clinic and down the hall again. We were stopped by a doctor in a white lab coat.

"Dave, how are you? I see you brought your little play pals to fight crime."

Warren said, "Well, Doc Morgan, I see you're still a little addled in the head from when Killian did a number on you."

"I'll just ignore you, Stevens. Dave, the woman had a severe blow to the head. It's lucky she didn't have a concussion." The doctor smiled at Warren and stuck his tongue out.

Warren laughed. "Good one Doc. Glad you're feeling better."

*

Chapter 11

Dave pulled Warren into the room before Doc Morgan could do more annoyance. "Will you grow up?" Dave said to Warren.

"Hey, he stuck his tongue out at me."

"Well, end it like a professional. You're a federal agent, act like one. God, I swear you haven't grown up since I've known you." Dave left him and went to the woman who was still eating.

Warren grinned at me and told Walt to follow Dave. Walt put his laptop on the table next to her bed and stood waiting.

Dave didn't say anything for a few moments, then finally he said to the woman, "I'm so sorry, I didn't get your name."

"Don't worry. I'm Nancy Gretchinson...I mean Harper, my married name." She started to tear up a little. Walt came to her.

"Nancy, I'm Walt. I'll try to help you remember what the suspect looked like and get a composite of his face so we can identify and catch him. Now I want you to relax, put your head back on the pillow and think back to last night when the man came up behind you. Focus only on his face. Forget everything around the area except the man. You can relax, no one can hurt you now, you are safe with us."

The woman closed her eyes, squeezing out a few tears. She put her head back on the pillow and went silent. Walt opened up the laptop and started the program. For the next half hour Walt asked her questions and did some work on the laptop. He continued to gently ask questions and occasionally asked her to look at the picture on the laptop screen. She said it was looking more like the man she saw. After another fifteen minutes Nancy announced that the picture was the man she saw. She was eighty percent sure it was.

"Good," Walt said and printed a copy from the portable printer he brought out of a case. He handed the picture to Dave.

"I know you can run off more copies. I'll have these passed out to my men and maybe someone will recognize him," Dave said. Walt ran a bunch more, adding the text to them saying this man was wanted, then handed the sheets to Dave.

Dave handed the sheets to Mike and said, "Take these to Virgil to pass out to the men watching the roads and post them any place people go. Let's get this face out before he leaves town."

Mike went out and Warren said, "Looks like you got this under control. Can I go see my favorite girlfriend?"

Dave smiled and said, "She's busy. She's shopping with a celebrity."

"Celebrity? Who?"

I said, "My wife, Penny Wickens."

Warren gave me a blank stare. "Who?"

Dave laughed and said, "You must be the only person in America who doesn't know Penny Wickens."

"Is she a movie star? I don't go to movies," he said.

Walt laughed and said, "She's a famous TV talk show host."

I looked at Walt. He said, "I had a lot of time on my hands before getting into the Seattle FBI. I watched a lot of talk shows."

"Okay, I'm not a big fan of TV. So I'll just say that I'm impressed," Warren said.

"You'll get to meet her, then you won't forget her," Dave said.

Nancy was resting now, looking at the sheet Walt had given her. "This is the bastard who ruined my wedding night."

"We'll get him, Nancy," Dave said. "I'll have every one of my people in town watching for him. It's just a matter of time."

"What makes you think my husband isn't dead?" she asked.

"We haven't found a body yet. Can you think of any reason the killer wouldn't just dump him in the woods by the campground?" I asked.

She looked at me and said, "I don't know. Is the killer taking my husband with him?"

"We don't know yet. If he is, there has to be a reason for it. What'd your husband do for a living?"

"He works for a pharmaceutical company. He's a chemist."

I felt a chill and looked at Dave. He had a shocked look and asked, "Does he know a man named Kenneth Laymen?"

Campground Murders

"I don't know. He never spoke of his work or his friends."

"While you were in the campground, did your husband talk to any other campers?" I asked.

"He did spend some time with a couple men. My husband likes to talk baseball and football. I just let him have his time with the men."

"My deputy never said that your husband mentioned knowing the dead man. You know which campsite the man was killed at. Was it one of the sites where your husband was talking to one of the men?"

She was silent for a moment, closing her eyes and thinking. "As I recall, it was. Jeffery went down there a couple times and was talking to a man on the road. They were looking at a book. I figured it was some sports book. I never asked when he came back. Should I have?" she asked.

"Hard to say, it may be nothing. I'll get a photo of the deceased and show you to see if it may be him."

"Is it important?" she asked.

"Could be very important, or nothing at all. We'll see. Now we'll let you rest. Thank you for helping with the sketch," Dave spoke softly to her.

Bob Moats

She put her head back and closed her eyes again. Dave signaled for everyone to leave the room. Walt had his equipment already packed and carried it out. Then Walt went off down the hall, I presumed to put his stuff back in the van. Dave, Warren and I stood just outside the door.

"Okay, we found a book of chemical formulas in with the effects of the dead man. Now we find that the missing man was a chemist. Did the killer plan this all out to murder the one man and take the other? This is baffling."

"Did you find out anything on the vic? Where he worked or what he was up to?" I asked.

"I'll have Virgil get on that. We'll see if there's a connection to both men, the vic and the missing man." Dave excused himself and pulled out his cell phone to place a call.

Warren stood by and said, "So you're married to a celebrity? You're a famous P.I. yourself and your wife is a famous personality. You must have a great life out in Vegas."

"Not really. At the end of the day my wife is just that, a wife. Have you ever been married?"

"Unfortunately, I have. It didn't end up so well. And she wasn't a celebrity. Although she thought she was," he said with a laugh.

"I've known my wife since grade school. She waited forty years to tell me she had a crush on me. We're making up for lost time." I liked telling that story.

Dave came back and said, "Nothing much left to do until we locate the suspect. Mike gave the sheets to all the men and they are watching closer now." He looked at Warren and said, "Sorry to drag you all the way out here. I don't know what more you can do. I just wanted Walt to do a picture of this guy to go on."

"No problem, I wanted to get away from Seattle anyway. I think I'll just get a motel room up at the north end and go fishing in the canal. That way I'll still be around to pull your butt out of trouble." He smiled and said, "Nice meeting you, Jim. I'll see you both before long." He laughed aloud and walked down the hall.

"He's a little crazy when he's not being nuts," Dave said. "Let's go to my station and get organized."

We went to Dave's car just as Mike was pulling up. He rolled down the window and said, "You want me to watch the woman?"

Dave thought on it and said, "It may be a good idea. The killer may try to use her to force the husband to do what he wants."

"I think you've got the right idea now," I said.

Mike drove off and parked. We got in Dave's car and drove out from the clinic.

"You're thinking that this suspect may be forcing the husband, Jeffery, to do something with chemistry? But we have the book. So what good does that do?" I said.

Dave said, "Maybe it's not the only book."

*

Chapter 12

We arrived at the sheriff's office to find Virgil just pulling up also.

"Any word yet?" Dave asked him as Virgil got out of his car.

"If there was, I'd have called you. Are you losing it?"

Campground Murders

"Sorry, Virg, I guess I'm a bit distracted. And a little hopeful. We've found out a new twist and I want to follow it up. Do you have the info on Laymen so I can check his background?"

"Sure, I got a few details already." He went up the front steps to the entrance and inside.

We got to the counter. I waited in front as Dave and Virgil went around to their desks. Virgil sat as Dave hovered over him. "I ran his license and got his corrected address. He lives in Olympia now, although his license said Tacoma. I called the phone number he gave on his change of license application and left a message. I didn't mention that he was dead, just wanted to talk to someone. Got no reply so far."

"Give me the number and I'll call," Dave said.

Virgil wrote down the number from the pad he had and handed it to Dave. Dave went to his desk and called. He signaled to me to come around the counter and sit. I did while he listened on the phone.

He waited and then said, "I'm Sheriff Chandler, Jefferson County Sheriff in Brinnon. I'm looking for a relative or spouse of Kenneth Laymen. It's very important, please call me back." He gave his phone number and then hung up. "Still no answer. I hope we have the right number and that he doesn't live alone."

"I'm going to call Penny to make sure she hasn't passed out from shopping," I said. Dave laughed.

"I'm sure Sarah will carry her if she does," Dave said.

I pulled out my cell phone and called. After three rings on my end, Penny answered. "Hey Sweetie, did you catch the murderer yet?"

"You have such faith in me. We're working on it. This is like following Deacon around on his cases. I watch and hope we get something on the killer."

"Are you contributing to the case?"

"We just started to gather information. Now we have to put it together."

"So you got nothing," she said with a slight giggle.

"I wouldn't say that. Now, how are you women getting along?"

"I love Sarah. I may divorce you and marry her. She loves shopping as much as I do. Plus she knows where the good deals are."

"Where are you guys?"

Campground Murders

"At a new strip mall. It has ten stores selling everything from dresses to shoes plus one that sells dollar things. It's got lots of good stuff," she said.

"Please remember how much room we have in the van. Where's Willy?" I asked.

"In the car with Van Gogh. They're so cute together. I think we'll have problems separating them when we leave."

"Maybe when we get back we can buy Willy a playmate," I said.

"I was thinking of a kitten."

"Are you serious?" I asked.

"We'll see. Now I have to go. Sarah just came out of the dressing room. She's modeling lingerie." She laughed and hung up.

"She can't try on lingerie, it's not allowed," I said to myself.

Dave gave me a strange look. "Who's trying on lingerie?"

"Penny said it was Sarah, but stores don't allow people to try on underthings. Sanitary reasons. Penny was just yanking my chain," I said as Dave's desk phone rang.

Bob Moats

He answered and listened. "Yes, I called. I'm the sheriff here in Brinnon. Do you know where that is?" He paused and then said, "Do you know Kenneth Laymen?"

He looked at me, nodded and continued, "Ma'am, did you know that he was camping in our campground?" He paused again. "Ma'am, I'm sorry to say that your husband is deceased. We are trying to find out what happened to him."

From my seat I could hear the woman crying loudly through the phone. Dave waited until she calmed. "I'm sorry to break this to you over the phone, but we weren't sure if you knew the man. I need to ask a few more questions, if you feel up to it?"

He listened and then said, "Can you tell me what line of work your husband was in?" He gave me a nod and then said, "Ma'am, may we visit you personally to talk further? I'd like to call a counselor to meet us to help you through this. Is that alright?" He listened and then said, "I have your address in Olympia, and we'll be there in about an hour. Please stay home until we get there. Thank you." He hung up and started to make another call. "I'm calling a friend in Olympia PD to see if he can send a grief counselor to this woman." He waited, then talked to his friend after waiting for him to come to the phone. Dave hung up and said to me, "Feel like a long ride?"

Campground Murders

"How long?" I asked.

"Well, it's about an hour to Olympia, then we'll be there about another hour talking."

"I think the women will run out of places to shop by then," I said.

"I have a better idea," he said and pulled out his cell phone. He hit speed dial and waited. "Hey, hon, would you like a trip to Olympia and maybe catch a nice dinner there?" He waited and said, "Meet us at the house." He hung up and said to me, "That's how you stay out of trouble with the wife. Take them along." He laughed and stood.

"Virgil, keep an eye out here and I'll be back later. Anything develops, call me," he told the deputy. We went out to his car and back to the house.

The women were standing in the drive waiting when Dave stopped. We got out and went to them.

Penny said, "Dave, do you always take Sarah on your cases?" She looked at me when she said that.

"Not really, this is just a fact finding trip. I hated to leave you two alone," he replied.

Sarah bumped his chest. "You just want to be sure I don't spend all your hard earned money."

"That, too. Now I'm going to see the widow of our victim so you and Penny can go to the mall while we talk. Then we'll go get something to eat. Can you follow us in your car?" Dave asked.

"If you don't drive slow like you usually do," Sarah said.

"I observe the speed limit. I'm not you." Dave smiled and told her to get moving.

We drove out of the drive and down the 101. The distance to Olympia was about 60 miles according to Dave.

"My friend said he'd have the counselor there before we arrived. I don't like telling people their loved ones are dead. I hope this woman takes it easy until we get there."

Dave's cell phone rang. He answered. "Hey, Barry, did you take the counselor to the woman?" He listened. "Good, is she alright?"

Dave told his friend Barry about the case and to keep the woman comfortable. We drove on.

About an hour later we pulled up to the house. Sarah and Penny with the dogs pulled up behind us. Dave went to Sarah and said, "You can go to the mall while I talk to this woman. I'll call you and we can meet at that Italian restaurant we ate at last month. How's that sound?"

Sarah reached up, pulled Dave down by the shirt to her in the car, and planted a kiss on his lips. Dave smiled and stood. "Okay, get lost. See you later." He came around the car, and he and I went up to the house. There was a police car in the drive, and a cop came out to meet us.

"Barry, this is Jim Richards, P.I. from Las Vegas. Jim, this is a buddy of mine from my days on the Tacoma PD, Barry Horst."

I shook his hand as Dave asked, "How's the woman?"

"Better with the counselor talking to her. I told her you'd explain the situation when you got here," Barry said.

"Thanks. I have a mystery. Her husband was murdered in our campground, and we have a man missing that may have something to do with it. I need to talk to the woman to see what her husband was doing there. I wanted to talk in person, not over the phone."

Barry nodded and said, "I understand, been there myself. Well, are you ready to meet her?"

*

Chapter 13

Barry took us into the house and to a living room. The house reminded me of my grandparent's home. It was old and decorated with knick-knacks on the walls. The furniture was from another era, the fifties I'd say. Either they didn't have much money or liked to shop in thrift stores.

The counselor was a woman. She smiled at us as we entered the living room. I stood by the opening to the room as Dave and Barry went to the woman sitting on the couch. I could tell she had been crying. It's hard to be told your spouse is dead and then be questioned by the police. I never liked this part of the investigative process.

Barry said, "Marge, this is Sheriff Chandler. He needs to ask you a few questions."

The counselor asked, "Marge, are you well enough to help the police find out what happened to your husband?"

The woman nodded and held a tissue to her nose and eyes. Dave sat on the couch next to her.

Campground Murders

"May I call you Marge?" Dave asked. She nodded. "I'm sorry about your husband, but it's my job to find the person responsible for his death. Can you tell me what line of work your husband was in?"

"You think it had something to do with his job?" she asked.

"We aren't sure, but I need to know."

"He worked for Emerson Pharmaceuticals. He was in research and development. It was his job to find chemicals to help people. He had a lot to do with people affected by mental disorders. A number of his drugs are being used to ease people with those problems."

Dave looked at me, then said, "Do you know why he was in the Brinnon campground?"

"Ken often went off to work on his formulas. Do some thinking to clear his head, he would say. I never knew where he went off to," she said with a sniffle. Dave handed her another tissue from a box on the coffee table. "Thank you. Sometimes Ken would go to a motel. I thought he was having an affair but I hired a private investigator, and he said that Ken was being faithful."

"I'll need that investigator's name later. How long would he go off for?"

"Sometimes days. He was gone one whole week once. I could call him on his cell phone but he never would say where he was. I was sure he was up to something, but the P.I. said he was just holed up and doing nothing."

"Did Ken ever mention a person named Jeffery Harper?" Dave asked.

The woman was silent for a moment, thinking. "I think he mentioned the name once or twice on the phone. I never listened to his conversations, but he didn't hide them either. It's hard not to hear things being said. The name is familiar, yes."

Dave thanked her and said, "I have to make a call, excuse me." He stood and came over to me. "This is getting interesting. I'm calling Mike at the clinic to ask the wife what company Jeffery worked at. We know he worked for a pharmaceutical company but not the name." He pulled his cell phone out and called. He asked Mike to check with the wife and waited. He listened then hung up. Dave smiled and said, "The same company as Laymen. They had to have known each other."

I said, "Probably why Laymen was in that campground. To meet with Harper."

"I'm seeing that, too." He turned back into the room, went to the couch again and sat. "Mrs.

101

Campground Murders

Laymen, I'm finding a link between your husband and this person named Jeffery Harper. They both worked for the same company. Jeffery Harper was kidnapped in our campground and his wife is in our hospital. She's alive, but we don't know where her husband is. They were attacked by the man we think may have murdered your husband. If you can think of anything you heard when your husband mentioned Harper's name, it may help."

The woman sat back on the couch and thought. "I heard Ken mention about some drug they were developing. But he never mentioned what it was. Only that they had to keep it secret. Or so he said. Could this be why Ken was killed and this Harper man is missing?"

"Possible. I need to investigate further before I can say conclusively. I really appreciate your cooperation and I'll be sure to keep you informed as to what we find out."

"Thank you, Sheriff. If I think of anything else, may I call you?"

Dave handed her his card and said, "Anytime."

He stood again and smiled at Barry. "Thanks, I need to get back to Brinnon." He looked at the woman counselor and thanked her also.

Bob Moats

We went back to the car and Dave sat for a moment. "Okay, they both worked for the same drug company. Were they working on something that got Laymen killed and Harper kidnapped?"

"Drugs are a big business. If Laymen was working on some new drug for mental illness, it could be worth lots of money to a rival company."

"You think a company would murder for a formula?" Dave asked.

"I've seen companies murder for less. We need to find Harper and the killer before they get away."

"I agree but first we have a dinner date with our wives or they will murder us." Dave smiled and started the car. He pulled out his phone again and called Sarah. He told her we were ready to eat. He hung up and drove out.

Dave was familiar with Olympia. He told me he had worked for the police there just before going back to Brinnon to become sheriff. He told me he was raised in Brinnon and had moved as far as Tacoma.

"I never went to Seattle, too big and too much crime for me. I like giving out tickets for speeding and jaywalking," he said with a laugh.

Campground Murders

"Interesting, because your town has been the site of three major crimes that caught national attention."

"I regret that happening, but it couldn't be helped. I'm glad everything went well. I understand your wife has been a victim in your crimes, just like my Sarah."

"Yeah, I'm the big shot detective, but she gets involved with my cases. Not that I let her, but it just happens."

"Oh, believe me, I understand. Here we are," Dave said as he pulled into the restaurant. It reminded me of Angelo's restaurant. We parked and got out to find the women standing by the front door.

"About time you got here. We're hungry," Penny said. "How was the interview?"

"Interview? You sound like you've been around police work." Dave laughed.

"When you're married to a P.I. and have nothing but police friends, you pick up on these things," Penny said.

"The interview was interesting. We have a few more leads as to the situation behind the murder and kidnapping. Still need to find the killer. Shall we go in and eat?"

Bob Moats

We went in and were seated. The place was very much like Angelo's. Even Penny mentioned it. We had a good meal, but I had to say not as good as what my daughter Carol could prepare. We finished and went back to the cars. It was now about five o'clock and we were wearing down. Dave told Sarah to be careful driving back. She smiled and peeled out of the parking lot.

"Is your wife as dangerous as mine?" Dave said with a laugh, watching her speed away.

I laughed back and said, "From what I've seen so far, they could be sisters."

We drove back to Brinnon and then to the station. Dave parked and we went in. Mike was at the desk, which surprised Dave. "Who's guarding Mrs. Harper?"

Mike replied, "Virgil. I think he just wanted to sit around. I got tired of it and let him. No word yet on the killer. He has to be hiding out in town somewhere."

"We've been here before with all the serial killers and terrorists. So how many places are left to hide?" Dave asked. "I'm not fond of searching every empty building in the area again. We need to keep track of them all for future attacks on our town."

"The road blocks turned up nothing and there have been no ransom demands for Harper. All has been too calm," Mike said.

I said, "The calm before the storm."

Dave looked at me and said, "I truly hope not."

*

Chapter 14

Mike said that since we were back, he was going out to patrol. Dave let him. We sat at Dave's desk and didn't say anything for a few moments. Dave sat way back in his chair. I thought he might go over but he balanced well.

Dave finally spoke. "So we have a dead man who was a researcher at a drug company. He gets murdered and another man who was also an employee of the same company is taken by the man we assume murdered the first man. Do you see a connection?"

Bob Moats

"They had to be working on something together. The wife of the missing man said the two men had talked. So they had to have something going on. We may need to go to Emerson Pharmaceutical and inquire as to what they were working on."

"We? Are you joining my task force now?" Dave smiled.

"You and I are the task force. Unless you want to include Mike and Virgil?"

Dave laughed. "No, they're good for writing tickets and such, plus they were good during the serial killer invasion. But they aren't much in the investigative vein. Okay, you can come along if your wife doesn't mind."

"Penny is used to me being off with the Las Vegas Metro PD chasing down killers. It gives her time to do her thing. Which is shopping, swimming or pole dancing."

Dave gave me a strange look. I said, "It's a long story. I'll tell you about it sometime."

"I look forward to it. Maybe your wife can talk my wife into pole dancing," he said. "Now we need to talk to the company they worked at, as you've said. What do you think they may have been up to?" Dave asked.

"Well, they may have discovered a cure for mental illness. That would be worth murdering them for the formula." I paused then said, "Maybe they were working on some synthetic designer drug that they could sell on the streets?"

Dave looked at me and said, "Now that's scary. Some drug lord would want that drug. Enough to murder one man and kidnap another. Maybe Harper had the details of the drug and the killer wanted him to work for the drug cartel."

"If Harper wasn't willing to cooperate, then his wife could still be in danger. She could be used to force Harper into doing the deed."

"Maybe I should put Mike on her also. Virgil may fall asleep on the job." He leaned toward the radio and picked up the microphone, calling Mike to go to the hospital and stand watch with Virgil. Mike acknowledged and signed off.

"Okay, we don't have much to do now. It's late and there wouldn't be anyone at the company now. Let's get an early start in the morning and see what we can come up with."

"Agreed. Shall we go see what the wives bought?"

"Agreed," Dave said and got up. We went out as Dave locked up the building. At the car I asked, "You don't mind us camping out on your lawn another night?"

"Nope, you should go get a refund on your campground fee. I'll talk to the manager."

I laughed. "I'm not worried about the money, but I don't want to intrude on your privacy at home."

"You already are, but that's no problem. My wife likes having your wife around. Besides, I'm using you to help solve this case. I hope you don't mind?"

"No problem, I enjoy intruding and helping with cases."

We drove out and to the house. Dave stopped at the General Store and we bought more beer. I had a feeling it was going to be a long night.

We found the women sitting out in the back by the canal. They had mixed drinks this time. I assumed they were out of wine.

"Sweetie, have you caught the killer yet?" Penny loved asking me that question. She knew I hadn't, but it was a conversation starter for us.

"No, my dear. We're working on it." I gave her my standard reply. "Have you stuffed all the things you bought into the van?" I asked.

"Yep, and I left a little room for you to drive," she said with her evil smile. I bent over and kissed her.

"That's nice of you. Sarah, are you and Penny playing nice?" I asked.

"We are. I may not let her leave. It will be so boring around here without her."

Dave came up behind Sarah and said, "So you're bored with me?"

"Yes, hon, you are boring. I don't know why I put up with you, but you are good for one thing."

"I don't want to know. It will involve sex, I'm sure," Dave said.

"See, you are a great investigator. Penny said you could go to Vegas and work for Jim." Sarah looked up at Dave and gave him a big grin.

Dave looked at me and said, "That would be interesting."

"I have two ex-cops working for me now. What's another? I'm fine with you working for the firm."

"I'll let you know," Dave said and laughed.

We grabbed a couple beers, pulled over deck chairs and sat. Penny reached over and took my hand, holding it tight. Willy came running up and bounced on my leg. I reached down with my free hand and picked him up. Van Gogh came up to my arm and watched me holding Willy.

"Don't worry, Van Gogh. I'm not going to hurt your little friend." The large dog sat and thumped his tail on the ground.

I stared out at the Hood Canal, just enjoying the scene. The moon was full and shimmering off the water. It looked dreamy. Penny squeezed my hand hard enough to make me look at her. "Hey, that hurts."

"Oh, big strong P.I. and I can make him hurt. I'm honored," she said.

Sarah spoke. "So are you two going on a hunt tomorrow for the killer?"

Dave said, "We're going to visit the company the victim worked for and see what he was up to. It may be nothing but it could be important."

"So I guess Penny and I will have to go shopping again tomorrow," Sarah replied.

Campground Murders

"Oh, good, I had a great time today. We need more clothes," Penny said.

"You two can do whatever you want. We have a murder to solve." Dave looked at Sarah. "You don't want another killer spilling blood all over your carpet, now do you?"

"You'll clean it up if they do. Why don't you call Warren in on this?" Sarah asked.

"I did. Well, I called Walt in to do a mug sketch, and Warren came along."

Sarah sat up and turned to Dave. "So where are they?"

"Right now I assume they have a room at one of the motels up on the north end," Dave said.

"And you didn't offer them our hospitality to stay?"

"Warren said he wanted to fish. You know him and his fishing. I figured he wanted to get away from the FBI and relax. I'll see him again and make him an offer to stay here."

"Well, you better." Sarah turned to Penny and said, "Warren is a friend and FBI agent who helped with the serial killers we had. If he's here, we can be sure we'll be safe."

"Hey! I can protect you too, you know," Dave said.

"Yes, but you are so slow in doing that. I could be dead before you did anything."

"I'm not even going to comment on who shot Max Draegon just before he tried to plunge a knife into you. It was my quick actions that saved your cute little butt."

Sarah sat back and smiled. "Okay, I'll give you that one."

We sat talking about anything that came up. Around midnight I said that I was getting tired, and Penny called me a wuss. I agreed. I stood and said to Dave, "Call me in the morning when you are ready to go. Just bang on the side of the van." I looked at Penny. "Don't you sleep with your gun tonight. I don't want you shooting Dave."

I pulled Penny up and we said our good-nights then went around the house to the van. Inside I set Willy on the floor. He went to his bowl. "I'll be right into bed after I feed the dog and let him take a dump."

He ate and then I let him out to do his thing. I looked up at the sky full of stars, took a big breath of the night air and smiled. Even though there was a murder, I was enjoying myself.

*

Chapter 15

Sleep came easily. It was quiet in the country. I woke early. Penny was still asleep so I didn't bother her. I went out of the bedroom portion of the van and closed the door behind me. I went to the small kitchen and took out the loaf of bread to make toast. I ate the toast and then got dressed.

I was watching out the window towards the house when I saw Dave coming out. I went to the door of the van and stepped out into the chilly morning. Willy followed me down his little steps.

"Good morning. Quiet night, I hope?" I asked.

"I called Mike about twenty minutes ago, and he said there was nothing happening. All the road blocks proved to be useless. I think the killer is still in the town somewhere. I called Warren and he was out fishing. He said when he caught his limit he'd be around to help."

"What's he going to do with the fish?" I asked.

"He'll probably give them to Sarah. She loves fish. I can tolerate it. I grew up in a family that lived on fishing the canal. I can take it or leave it. Shall we get ready to start our day?"

"Sounds like you already have," I said with a grin.

"I'm an early riser. I'm better in the mornings than later."

"I would prefer to spend my time in bed in the morning. But back home, duty and Penny call to me. I'll let Penny know we're going." I went back into the van as Dave went to the house. I fed Willy to keep him busy then went to the bedroom. Penny was up and dressed already, which surprised me.

"You're quick. I was outside for only a few minutes," I said.

"Sarah called on my cell. She's ready to start the day hitting the stores. She said we may go back to Olympia to go to the better stores."

"Well, be careful. Dave and I are going to a drug company to investigate our victim."

"Drug dealer?"

Campground Murders

"That's what we need to find out."

"You really enjoy murder, don't you? You love the chase," she said.

I thought for a moment. "I don't enjoy murder, but the chase is good. I like to bring justice and comfort to the victims. Helping people gives me a sense of accomplishment."

"You are such a saint," she said with a laugh.

There was a knocking on the door, and I went to open it. Sarah was standing there.

"Good morning. Are you ready to buy out the world?"

"I don't want the world, just the United States," she said. "Is Penny ready?"

"I am," Penny said from behind me. I got out of the way before she shoved me out of the van. She went past me and down the steps. Willy followed her down, and Penny picked him up. Van Gogh yipped at him, and Willy yipped back. The women said good-bye and went to the Vibe that was Sarah's car.

I cleaned up the van a little and then Dave came to the door. "I'm ready if you are. I think we'll go by the clinic first to talk to the wife."

Bob Moats

"Sounds like a winner," I said.

We drove out and headed to the clinic. "Where is this pharmaceutical company?" I asked.

"Not sure. That's one reason I'm going to talk to the wife. She would know where he worked. I'm hoping it's in Olympia. I don't feel like a long trip to Tacoma and definitely not to Seattle."

"The victim lived in Olympia, didn't he? I thought I heard the wife say that," I said.

"I guess so. Hopefully he worked there, too."

We arrived at the clinic and parked. Mike was sitting at the door of the wife's room. He stood when we came up.

"Where's Virgil?" Dave asked.

"He is sleeping in the extra bed in the room. We've been up all night," Mike replied.

"Well, then, take turns sleeping, but both of you stay by the wife. The killer may still try something."

"No problem. We've already worked out a schedule to nap," Mike said.

"Good, is the wife awake?"

"I couldn't say. I didn't want to bother her by going in."

Dave went past Mike and into the room. The woman was sitting up in bed reading a magazine. She smiled when she saw us. Dave peeked behind the curtain to the next bed and saw Virgil sound asleep. He went to the woman and I followed.

"Good morning. Hope you slept well," Dave said, standing next to her bed.

"Thank you, I did. Have you heard anything about my husband?" she asked hopefully.

"Sorry, we're still searching. I'll let you know if we find him. Now I have a couple questions. Do you feel well enough to talk?"

"Sure, if it will help."

"Okay, you and Jeffery live in Olympia, correct?"

"Yes, he moved there from Oregon about a year ago. I came out here to get married. Jeff's job brought us here."

"Does Jeff work in Olympia for the drug company?"

"They have a research center there. It's huge and has many employees."

"Do you know his supervisor's name?"

"I think it's Dickson. As I said before, Jeff didn't talk a lot about his job, and I didn't care."

"Dickson? Okay, thank you. We'll let you rest." Dave looked at me and nodded. I followed him out of the room, and he stopped to talk to Mike.

"Keep a watch. Let me know if anything changes. Do you have the search team men still hunting for him?"

"Yep, there are now ten guys doing the rounds. I deputized them, too."

"That's not official, but it will help them to do a good job. Call me if anything happens. We're going to Olympia."

We went back to the car and drove out. We were driving down the 101 as we talked about my cases in Las Vegas.

"Do the Vegas police let you ride along on their jobs?"

I laughed. "Well, I sort of have a good standing with LVMPD. I help and they take the heat. I've been deputized myself. Police auxiliary, which is how I get away with being involved. My best friends are a lieutenant and a sergeant in homicide."

"Helps to have people on the right side," Dave said.

We talked more, then we got to the border of Olympia. Dave stopped the car and made a call on his cell. He talked to Barry again. Dave asked if he knew where Emerson Pharmaceutical was. He listened then said he'd meet him there.

"Barry is going to meet us at his precinct and lead us to the building. It's a little complicated to find, he said."

We arrived at the police station and found Barry standing next to his car. "Do you get mileage driving back and forth from Brinnon?" he asked as we approached.

"Hell, I barely get paid, let alone mileage." Dave laughed.

"After you called me I made a call to our drug task force to ask if they knew anything about Emerson. They've been watching them for supposed drug dealings in Tacoma based on what an informant said, but they have no proof."

Dave looked at me and said, "Maybe your theory about the synthetic drug is a valid point. Our murder in the campground may have something to do with it." He looked back at Barry and said, "We have a researcher from Emerson missing and another dead. Sounds suspicious to me."

"I'm sure our task force would be happy to know about your case. I'll have someone call you later."

"Sounds good. Now can we go? Our wives are shopping somewhere in town and I'd like to get this taken care of as soon as possible before they spend all our money."

"Well, then that is an emergency. Follow me." He got into his car as we got into ours. We followed him out. The trip didn't take long, just all over the place and down numerous roads. We finally arrived at a large building out in a secluded area surrounded by woods. It looked sterile and foreboding. We parked and went in, followed by Barry. Dave thought it would be better to have a local cop on hand.

We went to the receptionist, and Dave said, "Good morning, may we see Mr. Dickson?"

She asked us what was the nature of our business with Dickson.

Dave said, "It's about the murder of one of his employees."

Chapter 16

Mr. Dickson was a very short, not-so-attractive man. Okay, he was ugly. I wondered if he took his own drugs and became deformed. He came to us and held out his hand. It looked misshapen like he had a childhood ailment or birth defect. I took it reluctantly, but admired him for not caring what people thought.

"Mr. Dickson, I'm Sheriff Chandler, Jefferson County sheriff out of Brinnon. This man is Jim Richards, private investigator, and this man is Officer Barry Horst, Olympia police," Dave said, pointing to us. "Are you are the boss of Kenneth Laymen?"

"I am. Is he in trouble? I knew he would get in trouble with the law. I just knew it. What did he do? Sell drugs? He had too much access to our stock, I knew he'd go bad," he ranted.

"Mr. Dickson, take a breath, please. Mr. Laymen is dead. He was murdered," Dave said.

Dickson went pale. "How? Was it a drug deal gone bad? Did he suffer?"

122

Dave stopped him before he went on. "He was murdered while camping, and we suspect another employee of yours is involved. Do you know Jeffery Harper?"

Dickson was pale again. "Yes, Jeff is an employee. He's a valuable employee. How was he involved?"

"May we talk in private?" Dave asked.

"Of course, follow me."

He took us down a couple hallways to an office in the back. It looked out through windows to a much larger room filled with people and equipment like something out of a science fiction movie. He stood at the windows watching the people.

"These are my people. All of them. Going to save the world, they are. They toil over their beakers and test tubes to find cures for all types of diseases. They will save the world and make Emerson rich." He stopped as he realized what he just said. "Of course we want to find cures, money is not our goal."

"Of course not," I said with a smile.

Dickson turned his attention to us. "So how is Jeffery involved in the murder of Laymen?"

Campground Murders

"We're not sure yet. That's why we're here. Jeffery Harper was kidnapped and his new bride attacked. We recently pieced together the fact that they both work here, and we need some information to help us. What exactly were Harper and Laymen working on?"

"Well, that's classified as company secrets. They were part of the research team involved in a new project. One that could help mental patients."

"Would this involve psycho-inducing drugs?" I asked, not really knowing what I was talking about. But it sounded good and might stir up the man.

"If you are talking about mind expanding drugs like LSD, they are close, yes. They help the mental patient to expand their minds and allow doctors to find out what is the nature of their condition. That's all I can tell you. You are versed on drug interactions?"

"No, just a hobby," I said, trying not to smile.

"Strange hobby," he said. "I can't help much more on the progress of the two men. As I said, it's confidential."

"Did they work together in the same department?" Dave asked.

Bob Moats

"They had connections through their research, but in different areas. Laymen worked on the creation of the drugs, Harper worked on the testing of the drugs. They worked closely but apart."

"Do you think they might have wanted to take their findings of the drug out of the lab and into the streets?" Dave asked.

"If you are asking, would they become dope dealers, they very well could. My concern was not just on the new drug they were developing, but on the drugs we already have on hand. I was going to have an audit done to check our supplies for missing drugs. The two men took vacation time off before I could initiate an audit. I thought that was strange, but not suspicious. Now I'm wondering."

Dave looked at me and said, "I think I may have to pull Warren into this. Head it off."

"If he can tear himself away from fishing," I said with a smile.

Dave tried not to laugh. "Okay, Mr. Dickson, do you really think either man could be capable of selling drugs?"

"I'm not sure of anyone nowadays. I have twenty-six people under my command. Three of them in the last six months have tested positive for drug use. We had to let them go. It hurt our progress.

125

Some of them were valuable employees. But company policy must be adhered to. I never could believe they would do such things."

"Did Harper or Laymen ever test positive for drugs?" I asked.

"That's the thing, they didn't. Nothing in our tests, not even alcohol. They were shiny clean."

Dave paused. I waited. "Okay, I think we have enough. May I call you if I have more questions?"

"Of course. I'll try to think of anything that may help."

Dave handed the man his card and said, "We'll be in touch if we find anything involving the men and drugs."

"Thank you, Sheriff."

Dave signaled us to leave. We went back to the parking lot and stood by our cars. "I think this is involving drug dealings now. We need to find out who the killer works for," Dave said.

"Or if he works for himself. Could be an independent wanting the drugs for himself. Brinnon doesn't get much drug trade, does it?" I asked.

"No, not really. We have next to no problems with drugs. Even the young people who live there haven't been caught with drugs. Drinking is another problem. They do like to drink," Dave said.

"Maybe we need to talk to a few young people to see if anything new has come into Brinnon. There had to be a reason for Harper and Laymen to be there. I'm sure they could have gone to a campground around Olympia," I said.

"True, it's something to look into. Shall we go back?" Dave thanked Barry for his help and we got back into the car and drove out.

"Do you have a connection to any drug task force in the State Police or Tacoma PD?" I asked.

"I don't, but I can call and see who is in charge."

"Might be a good idea to see what gangs are running drugs in this area. May be able to figure which one is responsible for the murder if this is a drug related crime," I said.

"I'm suspecting it is. All this is coming down to the connection between Harper and Laymen. They both work for a drug company and had something going on."

Campground Murders

We drove on just talking about nothing much in general. Dave was asking me about life in Las Vegas. I was asking about life in the country.

"It isn't like the big city. We don't have all the amenities you have. But we are close enough to Olympia and Tacoma if we need things like toilet paper. Those pine cones can sure hurt your butt," Dave said with a grin. "Plus we have mild winters up here."

"I'm originally from Michigan and I never liked the winter or snow. Vegas is hot, but I don't mind. I'm usually in air conditioning anyway."

"I could never figure how people complain about the cold in winter and yet in summer they turn their air conditioners down to nearly freezing. Doesn't make sense," Dave said.

"It's all in the head. As a species, we are messed up. You have your good people and your bad people. Then you have your politicians. I'm still not sure where they are in the spectrum of things."

We arrived back in Brinnon, and Dave drove to the station. The building was still locked since Mike and Virgil were guarding the Harper woman.

"I really need someone to man the station. That intern idea you had may be helpful." He opened the door and we went in. Dave went to his desk and sat. I wandered around the place then studied the wanted posters on the bulletin board. I heard Dave on the phone.

"Warren, it's Dave. Are you still on the canal?" he said then listened. "Good, can you come in and give us a little help? Oh, and Sarah said you need to stay at our place. She misses you." He paused, listening, as I went to sit next to his desk. "Great, see you then."

He hung up and said to me, "I'm calling in the Marines."

*

Chapter 17

About twenty minutes later Warren rolled into the station. He ambled up to the counter and leaned on it. "So what do you need from me that you can't handle?"

"The day I can't handle something you can is the day I retire," Dave said back. "We need some info that maybe the bureau can give. How up to date are you with your drug task people?"

"Still taking care of business. What do you need to know?"

"Who's running drugs in the area?"

"Well, Walt is out in the van communicating with the boys back in Seattle. I'll see if he can get the info for you. You want just the name of the gangs or all details?"

"Whatever you can get to track our killer. I'll explain when you get back."

Warren went back out to the van as Dave and I sat waiting. Dave called Mike to see how they were doing at the clinic. He talked briefly and then hung up. "Seems the clinic says Mrs. Harper is well enough to travel and they need the room. I'll have to figure where to put her until I think it's safe to let her go."

"Got a spare room in your house?" I said with a smile.

"With Warren and Walt, I'm afraid we don't have the extra space for another boarder. You got room in the fancy van of yours?"

"If she doesn't mind sleeping in the passenger seat." I laughed.

Warren came back in carrying a folder. He was followed by Walt. Warren came around the counter and pulled over a chair to us.

"Walt was busy. He sent a copy of the sketch to our lab and they did a search. Came up with this." He handed a sheet of paper to Dave. It had a photo and rap sheet on our mystery man.

Dave studied the paper and said, "Dominic Fresard is his name and he has a list of criminal activities that go back to 1968. Mostly drug running in the last five years. Reportedly works for the Grisdella mob out of Seattle." Dave looked at Warren and asked, "Is this mob still active?"

Walt spoke up. "They have been under surveillance for the last two months since they started to expand their grip into outlying areas. Tacoma and just recently into Olympia."

"Looks like they are eyeing Brinnon," I said.

"Well, they wanted Harper for some reason. They had to follow him down here and stake him out. Maybe Laymen didn't cooperate with their needs and so they canned him. Harper may have what they need."

"Dickson said that they thought someone was stealing drugs from the company. But would it be enough to distribute over such a wide area?" I asked.

Campground Murders

Dave said, "From what I understand, these men were involved in the manufacture of drugs. Like you said earlier, maybe they had a synthetic drug that the Grisdellas would want."

Warren said, "I could get some help from the Organized Crime Unit to see if they'd help finding Fresard. We could do another search of your modest little town. This would be, what, the third time?"

"You should know where all the good hiding places are by now," Dave said.

Mike came walking into the station and stood at the counter. "What do we do with the woman?"

"Where do you have her?" Dave asked.

"Virgil is watching her in the patrol car."

"Take this photo out to her and see if it's the guy she saw." Dave handed the sheet to Mike and he went out. We waited.

Mike came back in and said, "She says it's positively him. What shall we do with her now?"

"Why don't you and Virgil go help her pack up her campsite then bring her and her car back here? We'll figure what to do then."

Mike acknowledged and went out. Dave sighed "I just wanted to be a sheriff in a quiet country town. I just may move to Vegas for a rest."

"Penny and I have a guesthouse you can stay in," I said.

"Deal. After we catch this Fresard, I'm outta here." Dave laughed.

"Hey, if you move, where will I stay when I visit?" Warren asked.

"Sleeping bag on the floor," Dave said.

"No thanks, been there, done that," Warren said and stood. "I'll take Walt out and get some troops down here. We need to get this guy before all hell breaks loose with the mob." He took Walt and they left.

"I need to call Penny to make sure she hasn't bought any property out here." Dave laughed as I got out my cell phone and called. I stood and went to the other side of the counter. I wandered over to a door and looked in. There were jail cells in the room. I turned away as Penny came on the phone.

"Hey babe, how are you two doing?" I asked.

"Good. We're at the house and I'm showing Sarah how to make Shepherd's Stew."

Campground Murders

"Is that what we're having for dinner?"

"If it turns out, yes. If not, we eat out."

"Well, expect company. Dave has his FBI friends staying at the house for a night or two. Depends on how long it takes to catch our suspect."

"Well, we made a lot of Shepherd's Stew. So the more the merrier. What time do you think you'll be back?"

"Don't know. Warren is calling for reinforcements to help find our missing men. Keep the pot heating. I'll call before we come back."

I hung up and went back to Dave. "The girls have cooked up a surprise for us. But it's a good surprise."

Warren came back in and said the troops would be in later tonight. He handed Dave a stack of copies of the photo and rap sheet on Fresard. Dave thanked him.

We sat talking for about an hour before Mike, Virgil and the woman came in. Mike went to the counter.

"We tore down the campsite and then went to Laymen's site to take down his tent and put everything in his car. I had to hotwire it, then I drove it here and Virgil followed. Mrs. Harper followed us. What do we do now?" Mike asked.

Dave stood and went to the counter. He looked at Mrs. Harper and said, "How are you feeling?"

"I'm all right, but I'd be better if Jeff were here," she replied.

"I understand. We're having the FBI come in to help in the search for your husband. Now we need to find you a place to stay until this mess is over," Dave said.

Warren said, "Since it was her husband who was kidnapped and that comes under the jurisdiction of the FBI, I can get a motel room for her paid for by the Bureau. As a material witness under protection, I'll have a couple of my men watch her when they arrive."

"Great, Warren. I'll have Virgil take everyone to our best motel and get a room. That'll be good since Mike and Virgil have been on duty for two days now."

"Walt, why don't you take Mrs. Harper and go get dinner? That will kill some time before our men arrive," Warren said.

Campground Murders

Walt acknowledged and took the woman out. Mike and Virgil were standing by the counter when Dave told them to go home.

"Just be back in the morning so we can search for our missing man," Dave yelled as the two men rushed out the front entrance. We heard them say something, but they were too far away.

"I'll say for as goofy as those two are, they do a good job," Warren said.

"Yep, they were very helpful with our crime wave," Dave said with a laugh. "Jim, how are you enjoying your vacation?"

I laughed hard. "Well, I can never get away from murder, but I will say this has been fun. Plus Penny told me in bed last night that she is really enjoying being with Sarah. I think they will become good friends even if we are a thousand miles apart."

"Well, I think Sarah is ready to move to Vegas from the way she acted late last night. So they may still be able to shop. I hear Vegas has tons of stores."

"They have every kind of store you could want. It's a paradise for shoppers," I said.

My cell phone buzzed and I excused myself. I went around the counter looking at my caller ID. It was Deacon.

136

"Sorry, Deacon, I already have a murder here. So you are on your own," I joked as I answered.

*

Chapter 18

There was silence for a moment, then he spoke. "Murder? You have a murder on your vacation? How'd you manage that?" I could tell he was holding back a laugh. Deacon was like that.

"Penny and I were camping in the van, and then we met the local sheriff and his wife. Somehow we ended up with a body in the campground. Now the sheriff and I are looking for the killer." I explained everything in detail and then said, "So we now have the FBI in to help with the search for the missing man. Otherwise all is peaceful."

"You and that stupid curse. Can't go anywhere without a murder, can you?"

"Nope. How's the baby doing?" I asked.

"Good, although I haven't slept very well at night with the baby crying. I took a couple weeks leave from the precinct to help Lynn get adjusted to this lifestyle. I knew it wouldn't be easy and there are no instructions on how to do it."

"If there were, they'd be in Spanish." I laughed. "Have you gotten used to diaper changing?"

"I put a chip clip on my nose. I've been to crime scenes where there were bad decomp smells, but baby poop is lethal. We were taught to breathe through our mouths to avoid smells, but this is just worse."

"How's Lynn holding up?"

"She wants to be back at work. We've talked about getting a nanny or hiring Earl's girlfriend Paula to watch the baby. Our hours are so crazy, it's hard to toss the baby to someone at two in the morning when we have a death."

"You may need a live-in nanny. Just make sure she's good looking," I said.

"Yeah, that will go over real well with Lynn. I stopped by your office to see how everyone was, and all is quiet. Earl and Trapper have cases and Buck has put Mac in charge of the security so he can get away from it all. I know Buck worked hard to get the business going. He does need a rest."

138

"Yeah, I used to enjoy working cases with Buck. I'll have to see if he wants to be part of the investigative side now."

"I'm sure he would. He looked a little lost when I was there the other day. So are you staying around Brinnon or going to Seattle?"

"I think we'll stay here for a few days. Penny is enjoying her time with Sarah, and I have a murder to help solve. Of course with the FBI here, I'll probably be ignored. These people seem nice though. I could get to like them."

"Just remember you have friends and family back here. Don't abandon us now."

"Never. Good to hear from you. I'll call if and when we leave here to come back. Penny's network show starts in a week and a half, so she has to be back there."

"Okay, see you then. Just wanted to touch base and make sure you're still alive."

"Tell everyone we're fine, and talk later." We finished and hung up. I stood thinking about my friends back in Vegas. It was nice to get away, but I already missed them. I turned back to the counter. Dave was talking to Warren.

Campground Murders

"Call from back home?" Dave asked.

"As a matter of fact, yes. Everything is falling apart without me there."

"Good to know you're needed."

"Any word on your posse?" I asked Warren.

"They should be rolling in anytime now. It's only two hours and fifteen minutes from Seattle to here. If they don't stop in Olympia for a coffee break," Warren said with a grin.

Warren was a lot like Earl. They both had that something about them that said secret black ops agent. I knew Earl had a past with the CIA, and he still had friends in the FBI. "Warren, do you know an Earl Daws?"

"Sorry, no. Should I?"

"Not really. He's one of my investigators and he used to be a Detroit homicide detective. He has a shady past with the CIA and has a friend in the bureau named Harold Kettering."

"Kettering, hell yeah, I know Harold. He's a go between in the bureau and the top people in Washington. He knows everybody and where the bodies are buried. Good friend to have."

"I've worked with him a couple times. He's gotten information for me on a number of cases. As a matter of fact, he helped a couple months ago with a murder of an important food critic in Vegas. Turned out the critic had connections to high mucky-mucks in Washington."

"You need info, you go to Harold. He knows all, sees all," Warren said with a laugh. "I worked with him once. It was a new terror cell starting out in Virginia. The idiots were camping in the shadow of the FBI training center at the Quantico Marine Corps Base in Virginia. Didn't take long to find them after Harold did a little fact finding."

Dave's desk phone rang. He answered, listened and then hung up. "That was Eldon, one of the men watching the roads. They had a spotting of our suspect. The men who were watching the south road out of town spotted him in a car. He realized they saw him and drove back towards town. The men aren't police and didn't think they should give chase, but we know what the car is now, and that he's still in town."

"What about Harper?" I asked.

"Eldon said they only saw Fresard. But Harper may have been on the floor or in the trunk. Hopefully," Dave said.

Campground Murders

"As soon as my men get here, I'll give them the heads up on the car. But Fresard may ditch it now that he's been spotted. At least Fresard may have to hole up here now. He's been seen and knows we are watching the roads," Warren said.

"I'll tell the men to search every vehicle going out of town. Fresard may hide in a semi-truck or some other such vehicle," Dave said.

"If Fresard is still hauling Harper around, it may make it difficult for him to move freely. That could be bad for Harper," I said.

"If Fresard really needs Harper then it will be a necessity for him to keep Harper alive. I wish your men were here so we could start our attack. My men are good at helping, but they aren't trained to take Fresard down. I'm worried about them doing what they are. Fresard has already murdered one man. I hope he doesn't start shooting my men," Dave said.

We heard the entrance door open, and Penny and Sarah walked in. "I thought you were cooking at the house?" I asked Penny.

"We were, but the stew is in a crock pot so it's safe to leave alone," Penny replied.

Sarah laughed and said, "I didn't even know I had a crock pot." She looked at Dave. "It must be something you brought from your place."

Dave stood and came to Sarah, kissed her on the cheek and said, "Yes, dear, it was mine, and I used it a lot."

"What other surprises do you have in our kitchen?"

"I'll give you a guided tour later. Now you two need to be careful. Our murder suspect has been spotted, and he's still in town," Dave said.

Sarah lifted her jacket showing the gun Dave bought her for protection. Dave laughed and said, "I regretted getting you that concealed carry license. But this may be a good time to have it."

"Would you arrest me if I admitted I had my .38 in my purse?" Penny asked Dave.

"Do you have a permit to carry?"

"I do. It's good for Vegas and Nevada though," Penny replied.

"I won't say much about it then. Now just be careful. What are you doing here anyway?" Dave said to Sarah.

"We came to see what was happening. I see you are just sitting around while crime goes on."

"We're waiting for Warren's men to arrive to start a full attack. They should be here soon."

"Ah, the real crime fighters. I suppose you'll guide the attack safely from here," Sarah said with a big grin.

"Either Sarah is learning from you to be sarcastic or she's a natural," I said to Penny.

"Hey, this girl is talented and has a mind like mine," Penny said.

"Now that's scary, two of you," I said. Penny whacked me on the arm.

*

Chapter 19

Walt came back into the station with the Harper woman. He took her to the small breakroom off the side and came back to the counter. "Hey, Sarah, how are you doing?" he said, seeing her.

"I'm good, Walt. Have you shot any terrorists lately?" she said, remembering that Walt killed the terrorist who tried to sell a deadly virus on their last visit.

"No, none lately, but I may have another chance." He turned to Warren and said, "I got a call from Taylor in OCU. He had some interesting facts to tell us. Seems they have an informant who was following the Grisdella mob and it seems that Fresard has switched mob sides. He's no longer working for the Grisdellas. He is now in the employ of a mob out of Vegas. Don't have a name yet, but the informant said Fresard went out on his own to take persons unknown to the head of the Vegas mob regarding a new drug."

Dave looked at me and said, "Well, this just gets more interesting, doesn't it?"

I asked Walt, "They don't know what mob in Vegas it is?"

"Not yet, just that it's a newer gang that's forming in Vegas because of all the people and money to be plucked there with a new drug."

"I'll call my friends back there and see what they may have. Vegas PD has a big Organized Crime Unit due to the mobs and gangs still trying to keep a hold on the city. Something you don't read in the travel brochures. Mostly gangbangers doing the drug thing, and they are backed by drug cartels out of South America. If Harper has developed a new drug, he would still be alive to give the formulas to the bad people. Plus if it is some new drug that can be manufactured, it may make the drug cartels a little angry to be cut out."

"Since we have that book with the formulas, they would need Harper. It's probably all in his head," Dave said. He turned to Warren. "When your men get here we need to go full out to keep Fresard from leaving the area."

"I'll call the team leader and see where they are." He went off around the counter to make a call.

Dave said to me, "Interesting that you showed up here by mistake and then our crime spills over to your home turf."

"Really, Dave, I didn't plan it like this," I said with a smile. "I wanted to get away from crime."

Warren finished his call and came back. "They're a few miles out of town. Should be here shortly."

"Good, let's plan our attack," Dave said.

Penny and Sarah said they were not interested in our festivities. Sarah warned that she had a dinner at home. Dave gave her a blank stare. She laughed and said, "I'll keep it warm." They left.

Dave picked up the few copies of the rap sheet on Fresard and asked, "How many men do you have coming?"

"About fifteen. I'll have Walt run out some more copies." He asked Walt to do that and Walt went to the van.

About twenty minutes later, all of Warren's men were in the station and briefed on the crime. Dave gave them a heads up on his men watching the roads.

"They spotted Fresard but he ran back into town. We'll need a couple of your men with mine to do the law thing at the check points. I've got men from twenty to eighty years old helping to watch," Dave said.

"I'll assign a few of you to the roads. The rest will do a sweep through the town and the country side to see what they can find. Dave has sent out our flyers to the places in town where people congregate, so we may get lucky and they'll spot him."

Warren and Dave worked on getting the men out and searching. Walt and I stood watching the activities.

After the agents left to go search, Dave came to me. "If you can get a jump on this in case Fresard does get through our net, it would be a big help."

Campground Murders

"I'll call my people and get the thing rolling. Hopefully we can stop him here before he can leave town." I went off and pulled my cell phone out. I dialed Lynn. She at least could tell me what to do. Or she could get someone to call so I could explain the situation.

After a couple rings she came on. "This better be good, Richards," she said with a laugh. It sounded nice to hear her voice saying the words I had heard so many times before.

"Got a problem," I said.

"Is this about the murder where you are at?"

"That was the start of it. Now it's spilling over into a drug running problem that may end up in Vegas," I replied.

"Why us? Why not Los Angeles? Or San Francisco? Does it have to be Vegas?"

"You got the big money, and visitors like to get high on drink and drugs. I don't have the name of the gang yet, but can you get with OCU and see if they have any scuttlebutt on a new drug arriving? One that hasn't been seen before, just developed. I don't even have the information about it."

"How do you know about this drug?"

I went over the events of the last couple days, explained the kidnapping and the arrival of the FBI.

"Why don't the Feebies there get hold of the Feebies here and plan an attack?"

"They are, but I just wanted to get someone in LVMPD OCU to see what they may have. Those guys are closer to the streets than the Feds."

"True, they are in the front lines. I'll call a friend in OCU and have him call you. I don't really need any more homicides in the city over some designer drug."

"Thanks, I'll wait for his call. So are you adjusting to the baby?"

"Hell, no. It's a whole new world for me. I'm so used to being tough with criminals and now I have to be gentle with the child. I may ruin my rep out on the street," she said with a laugh.

"You always were a softie putting up a front. You'll do fine. Have your man call so we can shut this down."

"Okay, enjoy your vacation." I heard her laugh and she hung up.

I thought about calling Earl or Trapper. It might be a good idea. I dialed my office and waited.

Campground Murders

"Richards Investigation and Security, how may I help you?" Lacey answered. I wasn't sure if she didn't see the caller ID to know it was me.

"Lacey, Jim here, is everything okay there?"

"Yep, all is running smoothly, even without you." I missed her sarcasm. "Who do you want to talk to? Everyone is in."

"Okay, slow day?"

"Well, crime is down and husbands are not straying. Must be that you are out of town." She did it again. I smiled.

"Let me talk to Earl." I heard the phone click and then heard another familiar voice.

"Jim, how's life on the road?" Earl asked.

"Well, once I get past the murder and kidnapping it should be good."

"Kidnapping? Not Penny, I hope?"

"No, she's fine. It's a complicated story," I said and explained it to him. He was silent as I talked, then I finished.

"Well, this is not good. So you think this Fresard may be heading this way?"

"From what FBI sources say, he might. Since I'm not there, can you do some checking around and see what you can come up with? Maybe even call Harold in on it since Warren and he are acquaintances."

"I'll drop the name and see if Harold hangs up on me." Earl laughed. "If this is an easily manufactured drug, it could be difficult to stop. Hopefully the way to make it isn't like having a meth lab in your garage. You don't know the effects or the dispersal of the drug?"

"I'm not even sure if this is a drug related crime. We have only a few leads to go on. Until we catch Fresard or free Harper, we won't know what we're up against."

"Okay, I'll call Harold and see what he can find. I'll scout around my sources and see if anything is in the pipeline," Earl said.

"Thanks, give me a call when you find out anything, no matter how small," I said.

"Just don't get yourself killed. The monthly reports are piling up and Lacey is threatening to mutiny."

"Thanks, I really needed to hear that. Later." I hung up and smiled.

*

Chapter 20

I went back to where Dave and Warren were talking at the counter. Dave asked, "What's happening on your end?"

"I talked to my friend in the LVMPD and she's going to have someone from OCU call me and see if we can find out anything. She'll have her people ready in case Fresard should make it out of town. I also talked to my associate Earl Daws and he's going to scout around his sources and will call Harold Kettering to see if he can help by getting the Vegas FBI involved since this will be a kidnapping across state lines."

"Well, we have it covered both ways," Warren said.

"I hope it's enough," Dave said.

~~*~~

Bob Moats

Penny and Sarah decided to stop at the General Store to stock up on wine for the long night. The women in the store all came alive when Penny came in. She was ready for them this time. Sarah scouted the aisle with the few selections of wine the small store had. It was enough to keep them happy for the night. Penny came up with a cart and they put the bottles in.

"I don't see any wine in a box," Penny said.

"This is a high class establishment," Sarah said, laughing. "Besides, the box wine is over by the cashier where all the winos can get at it easily."

They picked out some snacks and took the cart to the cashier. Penny grabbed a box of wine. "For the men," she said with a laugh. "Never can have enough."

"While they were standing at the register, a man came up and asked, "Excuse me, aren't you that woman from the talk show?" He had on a baseball cap, dark glasses and looked like he just came out of the woods from hunting.

"I did have a talk show, yes, thank you," she replied.

"I thought so. Nice to meet you." He glanced at Sarah and turned to go out.

153

Campground Murders

"That was strange," Sarah said.

"You meet all kinds. I get tired of being spotted every time I go out. I have no privacy sometimes."

"I can imagine that would get to you," Sarah said.

"In Vegas there are so many celebrities that I get lost in the crowds. That's why I like the city. You will have to come down for a visit sometime."

"I'd love that. We can go shopping for glamorous outfits," Sarah said with a smile.

They picked up the bags and the box and exited the store. Sarah had parked her Vibe near the side of the building since it was the only spot available. They put everything in the back and started to get in when the man in dark glasses came back up to Penny.

"Excuse me, I forgot to get an autograph. I hope you don't mind," he said.

Sarah didn't like this intrusion and came around the car to Penny. Just as Penny was taking the paper from the man he pulled a gun.

Penny saw it and said, "Crap, not again."

Bob Moats

"Alright, I won't hurt you as long as you two cooperate." He looked at Sarah. "Aren't you the sheriff's wife?"

Sarah didn't answer. "Good. You can come along also. Now the two of you move around the car to my van. Quickly and quietly. I've killed a number of people in my life. Your deaths won't bother me. Now move!"

Inside the store the cashier could see outside and saw what was happening. She pulled out her phone and called the sheriff.

~~*~~

Dave answered the phone and listened. He got a shocked look and then hung up. "Shit, Fresard has Sarah and Penny." He yelled for us to follow and headed to the door. Warren told Walt to stay with the wife. We went to Dave's patrol car and all got in. Dave sped out with sirens and flashers blasting.

We arrived at the General Store, and Dave pulled up to the door. We jumped out and went in the store to the cashier.

"Dave, I was just looking out the window when I saw this man taking your wife and the TV lady to some van. I called you right away."

155

"Thanks, Vivian. What color and make was the van?"

"It was a dark blue Ford. That's all I can tell you."

Dave got on his walkie-talkie radio and called to all the men on the road detail, telling them to watch for the vehicle. Warren called his team leader to alert the men about the abduction. I was ready to wet my pants.

"It seems he needs some hostages to make his escape," Dave said. "I'm surprised he got Sarah so easily with her gun tucked in her holster."

I wondered if there were any pipes in the van so Penny could smash his head in.

"You know now that he has the women, he has the advantage. With just Harper, we could have taken him easier, but this now is a situation. He can call the shots and get out of town."

Dave's cell phone rang, and he looked at it. It was Sarah, he said. He put it on speaker and answered, "Sarah?"

"Ah, she is your wife. Well, that's good. I thought the famous TV lady would be enough, but I just got the brass ring." It had to be Fresard.

"Fresard, you hurt either one of the women and your life is worthless!" Dave yelled into the phone.

"Now, now, Sheriff, let's calm down and listen to my demands. I want the road block south of town opened and all the men called away so I can drive out safely. If I see one Fed or one of your bumpkins with a shotgun, I'll have to make one of the women suffer. Who it will be is up to you. Now move those men!" He hung up.

"Damn, I have to do it. I'm not sacrificing either of our wives for this creep." He pushed buttons on his cell as he said, "Warren, call your men and have them get away from the south 101. We'll have to follow him the best we can." Dave talked to someone and told them to abandon the road block. Warren did the same.

"Okay, he'll be heading out as soon as he sees the men leaving. We need to move now, but carefully. I'm sure he'll figure we will follow, but it's the risk we have to take. He knows we won't do anything as long as he has the women. Let's go." He headed out the door, on the phone again. I could hear him explaining to Virgil what happened and asking him to go guard the Harper woman so Walt could follow in the FBI van. We might need it.

Warren called Walt, explained it to him, and said to track Warren's cell phone so they could meet later. We got into the patrol car and Dave sped out.

Campground Murders

"We're going to be highly visible in this cop car," I said.

"I know but we don't have much of an option."

"Warren, call your men and have them stall a bit. That should keep Fresard holding on. We can meet with the FBI van. It's not far from here. We can follow him in that."

Warren pulled out his cell phone and told his team leader to stall, pretend to have car trouble. Then he called Walt and said to meet them on the 101 just north of the road block.

We found Walt waiting about a mile from the road block. Everyone jumped out of the patrol car and got in the van. Warren commandeered the driving. Walt didn't object. Warren took off down the road.

We stopped just before we got to the road block. The last of the cars was leaving. We couldn't see the van that Fresard was sighted in, but that didn't mean he wasn't in the area.

We waited until the road was clear, then saw a dark van pull out from a Put-Put golf course and onto the road heading south.

"Got him," Warren said.

"Hold back, don't crowd him. This is the only road south so he has nowhere else to go," Dave said.

"It's an eighteen hour drive straight to Vegas unless he plans on stopping along the way," I said. I thought about the campground Penny and I stayed at. I didn't figure he would stop there.

*

Chapter 21

"Walt, get on the horn and call in our stealth helicopter to follow Fresard."

I looked at Walt and asked, "Can you track GPS on a cell phone with this equipment?"

"I can. What do you have in mind?"

"I have Penny's phone set to locate her by GPS if needed. I'll give you the code and number."

Walt handed me a pad of paper and I wrote the numbers then handed the pad back. Walt went to a wall of electronics and did some fiddling. He called the bureau and requested the helicopter then gave them the GPS fix to help track also.

"The helicopter will locate Fresard by Penny's cell. Hopefully Fresard hasn't tossed the phones out," Walt said.

"I'm sure he'll keep them to contact Dave if he gets sight of us," I said.

Walt adjusted his equipment and said, "I got their coordinates. Penny's phone is still active. They're just ahead."

Dave said, "Pull back then, if we can keep him on the radar. No sense in crowding him. Jim, call your friends in Vegas and warn them that he's on the move."

I pulled my cell out and dialed. Lynn came on and I said, "Guess what?"

~~*~~

Penny and Sarah were tied up in the back of the van. They didn't have their mouths covered, so they could still talk. They didn't say anything at the moment. Penny looked back and saw something move under a tarp. Then the tarp started to move off the person who was under it. Penny didn't know who the man was but figured it had to be Harper. He managed to uncover his head and shoulders. He saw Penny and smiled.

"At least I'm not dead unless you're an angel," he said.

"Are you Jeff Harper?" Penny whispered.

"I am. Who are you?"

Penny felt relieved that someone didn't know her. "I'm a friend. We're in the same predicament. What is this all about?"

He looked around his surroundings and said, "A coworker and I developed a new formula for a semisynthetic psychedelic drug. It could be worth billions if put in the wrong hands. Not easy to make. It needs a certain fungus that is expensive to get. But the end profits outweigh the cost of the fungus. This is not a garden variety recreational drug. It is highly addictive and will spread fast. People will love it and want more. The people who want this have deep pockets and can produce the drug in quantities. It will become epidemic."

"Do you know where we are going?" Sarah asked.

"I heard this guy talking to someone on his phone. We're heading for Las Vegas."

Campground Murders

Penny was shocked and said, "Are you shitting me?"

~~*~~

Walt had a call and said to us that the helicopter was in the air and tracking the car. I looked out the window to see if I could see the thing but couldn't. "Where is it?" I asked.

"Oh, you won't see it. The thing can fly high enough with long range video and not be seen. Thanks to your wife's GPS they can follow it all the way to its destination," Walt said.

"I'm sure she'll be happy to know that," I said. "It cost me extra to have it installed, but worth it."

We drove on in silence for about five hours, and it was getting dark. "I don't think he's going to stop," I said.

"If you had a million dollar cargo, wouldn't you want to get to your destination quickly?" Warren said.

"So you figure this is a drug related thing?" I asked.

"All the signs point to it. From all we know it has to be some drug. And this guy is going to a lot of trouble to transport Harper to his bosses."

I was looking out the window at the darkness going by and thought Penny was safe so far. I wondered how the arrival in Vegas would go. Dave wouldn't want his wife harmed, and neither did I, so we would do what it would take to see they were safe.

After another two hours, Dave said, "I think he's going all the way. Warren, when you get tired, I'll take over."

"I'm fine. Eighteen hours is nothing to me. I just hope Fresard doesn't fall asleep at the wheel and run off the road."

That wasn't a pleasant thought. I figured that Fresard was anxious to get to Vegas, so he'd hang in there. I remembered during my first marriage driving from Cape Cod to Detroit for fourteen hours just to get back from a disastrous honeymoon.

We had crossed state lines from Washington into California. Fresard just broke a federal law. Now he was entering Nevada, making it worse.

Walt said the helicopter had to refuel, so they would be out of touch for a short while. They went to a Federal base in Nevada and refueled, then got back in the air. They said that the GPS still was active, but fading. I thought that Penny might have forgotten to recharge her batteries. Great, so close to lose the signal.

The terrain was difficult to see in the dark, no lights out here in the desert. Walt and I dozed for a while, Dave and Warren staying alert. My cell phone buzzed and woke me. I answered. It was Lynn.

"So where are you?" she asked.

I said to hold on and asked Warren where we were. He said about an hour and a half out of Vegas. I told Lynn. "Have you found out anything? I didn't hear from OCU."

"They have been busy tracking down any word on gangs moving some new drug. It takes time to get anyone who has info on this to talk. Everyone is frightened of the drug cartel wanting to know about this drug. No one wants to say they know. We do have one lead. Seems a mob has moved quietly into town from New Jersey. The OCU boys are checking more on it. I'll let you know. Now where are you coming into town?"

"Don't try and stop Fresard. As long as he has Penny and the sheriff's wife, we don't want to jeopardize them."

"Penny is going to want to murder you after this is over. Or divorce you. She has to be getting tired of being kidnapped."

164

"I know, I know. I'll have to change jobs for sure now. Maybe I can be a greeter at Wal-Mart," I said with a smile.

"That would be safe," she said.

"I'll call you before we arrive in town. We have a super-secret helicopter following the van as long as Penny's phone holds out."

"Ah, GPS. I love that feature. We have caught a good number of criminals that way. Okay, call and we'll go from there." She hung up, and I sat back wanting to get this over. It was now almost seven in the morning. We had been driving all night and I wasn't feeling good.

Walt stirred from his chair and woke. He looked at me and said, "Are we there yet?"

"Close, about another hour. How's the helicopter doing?" I said.

He turned back to his devices and said, "They are still tracking, but the signal is getting weak. The cell phone must be running low."

I hoped it would hold out until we got to where Fresard was heading.

Campground Murders

I could see the skyline of Vegas in the distance as we headed down the highway. I felt good being back home, but not for this reason. I called Lynn, told her where we were and I asked Dave what to tell her.

"I have no idea yet. Hopefully we'll be able to find out where he lands and go from there," Dave said.

I related that to Lynn. We finished and hung up. I called the office and Lacey answered. "I don't have time to fool around. Penny has been kidnapped and I need to talk to Earl."

Lacey said nothing and connected me to Earl. "Jim, what's up?"

I explained to him everything and where we were. Earl said, "I talked to Harold and he's got the Vegas bureau on alert. I've talked to an Agent Greski here and he has people standing by. Is your new friend Warren with you?"

"Yes, he's here. We have the FBI helicopter circling above, getting a fix on where Fresard is going. If Penny's phone holds out."

"I'll hang in until you tell me what you want me to do. I've got Trapper and Buck standing by," he said and we finished.

I just hoped I could figure out what to do next.

Chapter 22

Around 8 a.m. Walt got the call from the helicopter. Penny's cell phone had died. They lost the signal. Walt confirmed that through his instruments. We had no idea where they were going now. And would Fresard need Penny and Sarah now that he was in Vegas? I was worried.

I called Lynn and told her. I gave her the last coordinates of the fix on the GPS. Then I called Earl and told him. Everyone was going to war on this. I guided my new friends to my office to get our plans together.

We came through the back door and I led everyone to the conference room where Earl, Trapper and Buck were waiting. They had a map of Vegas spread out on the table and I introduced everyone.

"Okay, guys, this is where they were last tracked before the phone died," I said, pointing to the map at a space around a small industrial area of Vegas south of the strip.

Lynn came flying in with Deacon in tow. "Whatcha got?" she asked. I went over what we had, and Lynn said she had everyone in the precinct standing by for a word from her.

Agent Greski walked in, and I introduced Warren to him although I didn't know the man. Earl actually did the greetings.

Greski said, "I have my agents standing by as soon as we are needed. If you'll give me the description of the van, I'll disperse my men in that area to search."

I told him what to look for and explained the hostage situation. Greski went out as Lynn called her people to start the search.

"We have over fifty people now out hunting for the van. Unless he pulled into a building, we may spot it," Dave said.

Walt said they had the helicopter still doing a fly over to see if they could spot anything. I looked at Lynn and said, "Can you get OCU to give up their info on mob holdings in that area? Any buildings they have an interest in?"

"I'll put a fire under them." She went out to make a call.

Lacey came in. She looked worried but said, "Can I get coffee for anyone?"

Bob Moats

I told her to make a big pot and keep it coming. She went out.

Trapper and Buck came to me, and Buck said, "Don't worry man, we'll find her. I have all my free guards ready to search as soon as I give them the info on what to look for."

"Talk to Warren, he has the info you'll need," I said and pointed to Warren. Buck went to him.

Trapper stood by me. "I'll hang with you until we get this taken care of."

"Thanks, my friend. I'm just so worried. But I can't let it stop me from finding this bastard."

Trapper smiled and said, "I can't understand why Penny hasn't shot the asshole yet."

That struck me as funny, and I had to laugh, just to let out the tension I was feeling.

"Thanks, Will, you always know what to say." I turned my attention back to the map. I looked closely and wondered where they could be.

~~*~~

Fresard had Penny, Sarah and Harper get out of the van and go into the building he parked at. It was a small building nestled in an industrial complex just

169

off of Paradise, south of McCarran Airport, below Sunset Road. There were a number of manufacturing buildings, and Fresard went into one of them with his hostages.

"Okay, I'm keeping you two alive for now. You can still be useful," he said to Penny and Sarah. He pushed Harper toward an office after locking the women in a small room. The room had no windows. There was a table with a few chairs. Otherwise it was empty.

"Okay, I didn't want to see Vegas this badly," Sarah said.

Penny stared at her for a moment then laughed. "I'm sorry you had to see my town this way. But when the cavalry rolls in and we are free, I'll show you a good time."

"You owe me big time for this," Sarah said.

"Hey, he's your criminal. He brought us here. I don't claim him."

The women stood looking at each other and started to laugh. "I know Jim will find us. Oh, crap, I just thought of something. Our dogs are back in the house."

"And the crock pot is still cooking. This is not good. If I had my phone I could call Virgil and have him go check on the house."

"Tell me, would you call for help first or call Virgil to check on the dogs?" Penny asked.

"Wow, that's a tough question. I think I would check the dogs first. I know we can handle Fresard."

"Yeah, well, we haven't done such a good job so far. He got our guns and purses, so we can't do much."

Sarah was studying the room, looking around and then she looked up. "Hey, they have fire sprinklers. Do you think they would set off an alarm?"

"If we had matches we could see," Penny replied.

"Well, Fresard took our purses, but he didn't check our pockets." She reached in and pulled out a disposable lighter.

"Why do you have that? You don't smoke," Penny said.

"If you remember, I had to re-light the pilot light on the stove when it went out," Sarah said.

Campground Murders

"Ah, yes. So we need something to start a fire."

"Can't you just hold the flame under the thing to set it off?" Sarah asked.

"I guess so. I've never had to set off a fire alarm. Of course you know we will get soaked by water when the alarm goes off."

"A small price to pay for our freedom," Sarah said.

"Or Fresard will get pissed and shoot us."

"That, too, but we'll overpower him in the rain," Sarah said with a smile.

"I like how you think," Penny said and pulled a chair over to just under one of the sprinkler units.

"You're taller than I am, you do it," Sarah said.

Penny looked up and said, "I guess I can reach it. Give me a boost."

Sarah helped Penny up on the chair and handed her the lighter. Penny stood up and held the lighter up, but was still not close enough to do any good.

"This will take forever. I have to get the lighter closer to the sprinkler head." She looked down at

Sarah and said, "Climb up here and I'll boost you up to light it."

Sarah looked at the chair and said, "Think it will hold both of us?"

"We can try. We have to do something."

Sarah climbed up on the chair with Penny's help. Penny said to grab on to her shoulders and she'd give Sarah a boost up. They struggled to get Sarah closer to the head. They almost toppled over but caught themselves before falling.

"We just aren't close enough," Sarah said.

Penny looked around the room and noticed the wall paper. It was some kind of fabric. She got back down from the chair and went to a part by the door where she saw the wallpaper was separating from the wall. She grabbed on and pulled. Sarah was surprised that it came loose. They both pulled until they had a good piece come off. Penny tore it away from the wall and rolled it up.

"Okay, this will either work or we are doomed." She held out the roll to Sarah who had the lighter and told her to light it.

"You know we have no way to put out a fire if we succeed in burning this," Sarah observed.

173

Campground Murders

"That's the chance we have to take. Now light my fire."

"Okay," Sarah said as she flipped the lighter and touched it to the end of the roll. It took no time in lighting and was flaming good.

"Well so much for flame proofing a building," Penny said as she held it up to the sprinkler head. About a minute later water was streaming from the three heads in the room, and a loud alarm was sounding.

Sarah and Penny were getting soaked but jumped for joy. Penny said, "Fresard may come through the door any second, we need to be ready."

Penny picked up a chair above her head and went behind the door, waiting. No one came. Then the door burst open and still no one entered. Sarah looked out the door and was grabbed by Fresard, hiding next to the opening. He yelled to Penny to come out or he would kill Sarah. Penny put down the chair and left the room.

*

Chapter 23

Fresard pulled Penny over to Sarah and held his gun to her face. "You're the smart TV lady. You probably figured out how to set the alarms off. Well, it didn't do any good other than get you two wet. The alarms are internal and have been disabled to go outside the building. So no one is coming to rescue you. Now move down the hall." He pointed his gun towards where he wanted them to go.

The alarms were still clanging as he got to a door and told them to stop. He opened it and reached around to a panel on the wall. He flipped a switch and shut off the alarms.

"Now I need to put you two where you can't do any more harm." He pointed to another door and they went through. They were in a huge open room as big as a hangar where there were many tables covered with devices which looked like they could do some sort of chemical experiments. Fresard took them to the other side of the room and put them in a caged area that had empty shelves. Probably for storage. He put a lock on the cage and said, "Now play nice with each other."

Campground Murders

He turned back to the tables and Penny saw Harper standing by. He came around the side of the table and Penny could see he had a chain attached to his ankle. Fresard went to him and said, "Now get on the formula, you have all the ingredients. Set up the first batch for our guests tomorrow. You know what will happen if you don't." Fresard turned and went out of the room.

Harper looked at the women. "I'm sorry you had to be dragged into this. I messed up by talking to the wrong people. Laymen and I got greedy and felt we could make a lot of money by selling the formula. We chose the wrong people to trust. Instead of a competing drug company, we got hold of the mob. Now poor Laymen is dead and I'm going to create an epidemic of drug addicted people. This damn drug can even be put in water and addict people. They'll crave it so much that they would even kill for it."

"How do you know this will happen since the drug isn't available yet?" Penny asked from across the room.

"I've tested this on animals, mice and monkeys. The reaction was fine for helping with illness, but the craving was terrible. It caused a pleasant high, and our animals all relaxed and exhibited calm feelings. Actually they became lethargic to a point. But when the drug wore off they became irritated and edgy. They would fight with the other animals until we administered the drug again. It was the only way to control them after the initial use."

"You knew this drug had potential for danger, yet you went and tried to sell it. What were you? Crazy?"

"No! We were working for a billion dollar industry and my take home pay barely took care of expenses. Then getting married, I had another mouth to feed. Laymen was in the same boat. We were tired of doing all the work, not getting credit and making shit for pay. Haven't you ever wanted to stick it to your employer? Haven't you ever felt less than good because you were underappreciated for what you do? I worked hard for that company. I even moved out of my home state to Washington State to do their bidding. I felt I deserved more. I'm not proud of what I did, but I just had enough."

Penny looked at Sarah and said, "I guess I can't fault him for that." They she turned back to Harper. "But I can fault you for trying to sell a dangerous drug."

"I know, but if we sold it to another drug company, they might have improved it. Our company was only wanting to get it out despite my warnings. They saw the dollar signs. I just talked to the wrong people when I was looking to sell. I didn't know the mob had people out looking for drugs to push."

Campground Murders

"What happened at the campground?" Sarah asked.

"We were to meet with Fresard. He was the advance person for the mob. I thought he was with a pharmaceutical company. He demanded to have the formula and didn't offer to pay us. Laymen struggled with him and he was murdered. Fresard took me captive and back to a cabin he rented. I could hear him talking to someone on his phone about the drug, and he was told to take me to Vegas where they had a new operation setting up to distribute drugs. My God, if this drug were given out there before the side effects were fixed, everyone in Vegas who took it would go crazy as it wore off."

Penny said, "Then why don't you mix up a batch that doesn't do anything? The heads of the mob will think it was all a hoax."

"Oh sure, and get myself killed. No, thank you. Do you want to die if they think it doesn't work? Fresard wants to prove it works with his demonstration tomorrow."

Penny couldn't think of anything to say. She turned to Sarah and said, "All we can do now is hope Jim and Dave find us. I'm sure by now they have half of Vegas law enforcement out looking for us."

"Warren probably has his FBI buddies helping, too. They'll find us," Sarah said.

"If we can stay alive until then."

~~*~~

I was standing in our lobby as people were coming and going. They had set up a command post in the conference room. Between the local police, Buck's guards, and the Feds, there was a lot of movement going on. All I could do was wait to see if anyone came up with something. Trapper stood by waiting for me to collapse. I told him I was all right.

"I'm trying to figure out what all this commotion is about. The kidnapping? The drug that's going to be sold to the mob? I don't remember this much activity when we had the dirty bomb loose in the city," Trapper said to me.

"I welcome all the help we can get," I said, "just to get Penny back."

I suddenly had a thought. What about Willy? I got a chill then went over to Dave who was talking to Walt. "Dave, do you know where Willy and Van Gogh are?"

He gave me a stare then processed the question. "Crap, I don't. I don't think Sarah would take Van Gogh with her to the store so that means the dogs are at the house."

179

Campground Murders

"And Penny said they had food in a crock pot. That was yesterday," I said.

"I'll call Mike and have him go check the house. I hope it didn't burn down." Dave pulled out his cell phone and called. "Mike, this is Dave. I'm in Vegas and we still haven't found Sarah or Penny. Now I need you to do me a favor. Go to my house and see if our dogs are there and shut off anything in the kitchen that's cooking," he said and listened. "Good, call me when you get there."

He hung up and told me, "He's on his way. I'm sure the dogs are safe and the crock pot can cook for days without harm. I know, I've left it running a few times myself."

One less worry I would have now. I turned to Lacey standing behind the counter, looking lost. I went around the counter to her. She had tears in her eyes, and she gave me a hug when I got to her. "Don't worry, we'll find her. There are a lot of good men and women out looking. It's just a matter of time."

She said, with her head on my chest, "I hope so. It would be so lonely around here without her."

"Hey, we'll find her. Now see if you can help anyone. Just keep busy."

She nodded and stepped back. Then she went off to the back where everyone was congregating.

Lynn came rushing from the back and called to Dave and me. "Jim, Dave! My people have spotted the van. It's going east on Sunset. I told them to hang back and watch where it goes."

*

Chapter 24

Warren came out also and said to follow him. We went out the back door and to the FBI van. We got in and sat as Walt was turning on his equipment to the local police band. We could hear the conversation that Lynn was having with the patrol car. I guided Warren out of the parking lot and onto Industrial Road. He turned on the flashers and sirens. We jumped onto the Boulevard and headed south towards the airport. I showed him how to get to Sunset and told him to shut off the sirens so not to spook Fresard.

I called Deacon who was with Lynn, and he said they still had the van in sight. It was heading east on Sunset towards Mountain Vista. He reported that it turned north on Mountain Vista. The patrol car was still following. I thanked him and hung up.

We got up to Mountain Vista and turned left. I was watching for the van, but saw a number of vans coming close to the make. "How do they know this is the van?" I asked.

Warren said, "When the report came in, the patrol car spotted the van first, then identified the driver as Fresard from the rap sheet. Walt, call and see if the police got a license plate."

He called and then told us the number. I was watching for it. Walt said, "The plates are registered to a Herman Gilroy of Brinnon."

"Herman Gilroy, I know him," Dave said. "I also know the van. Fresard must have stolen it after he was spotted in the car."

"Since you know the van, see if you can spot it," Warren said.

We drove on and then saw the patrol car that was following the van. Dave said it was the van just ahead. I called Lynn and said to have the car back off before Fresard saw them. We were tailing him now.

The patrol car turned off and we moved up a little. Walt said, "I just got a report that our men are advancing behind us. Lynn Carter said she is pulling back her people to let the feds take over."

"I wonder if the women are in the van," Dave said.

"Earlier Fresard was south of the airport, now he's driving out here. He may have dropped off his hostages and is going somewhere else," I said. "Walt, call Carter and ask her to have her men continue to search the industrial complex where they were last reported. Just in case."

The van made a right turn on East Harmon Avenue. We followed, crossing Boulder Highway, and then he turned into the Eastside Cannery Casino. He pulled into the parking lot and got out. We were watching from a safe distance. Fresard went into the casino entrance as we moved up to the van. Dave and I jumped out and ran to the van, looking in the windows. It was empty.

"Damn, he did drop them off," I said.

Walt got out of the FBI van and put something on the back end of the stolen van. "It's a tracking device so we can follow him back to where he has the hostages."

"Very good, let's get away before he comes out and sees us," Dave said.

Campground Murders

We went back to the FBI van and sat. "Now if we lose him, we can still track him," Walt said.

I smiled and said, "You know, Walt, you're pretty handy. If you ever get tired of the FBI, I could use a man like you."

Trapper said from the back of the van, "He can replace Earl."

I was a little startled. "Will, I forgot you were still following me. I'm sorry."

"It's okay. You had a lot on your mind. Uh, guys, Fresard is on the move," Trapper said.

We all turned back to the front and saw Fresard moving from the casino to the van. He got in with a package under his arm. He drove out as I called Lynn to explain the situation. Warren called to his men to have them back off and go down to the complex.

We followed him at a safe distance, Walt still tracking the device. This van was amazing for all it could do. "Walt, how much does this van cost with all the equipment?" I asked.

"Well, we managed to lose one back when we were in Brinnon, explosion that almost got me. They wanted us to pay for it, but then decided not to. I was told it cost a half million dollars."

Bob Moats

"Jim, can we get one for the firm?" Trapper said.

"Sure, if you're paying."

We drove behind the van until a car ran a red light and smacked into another car at an intersection. Fresard was still ahead, and we couldn't get around the accident. I called Lynn to report the accident, and she said she'd dispatch the emergency vehicles. Warren was trying to navigate around the accident. Fresard was far enough away so he turned on the siren and flashers to move up on the sidewalk and back on the other side. I could see a patrol car roar up and stop at the scene.

Once we were away from the accident, Warren turned off the flashers and siren. Walt still had a fix on Fresard, but we lost the visual.

Lynn called me and asked if we still knew where Fresard was. I said we did. She had all her unmarked cars and detectives patrolling the complex. I said I'd let her know what was going on when we knew.

We got back on Sunset and headed towards the airport. Fresard pulled into the commercial part of the airport and up to a building. We sat out on the road, waiting. Fresard took the package into the building, and we waited. He came out and got back into the van. He drove out and back on the road.

Campground Murders

Warren waited until he was gone and then drove into the lot by the building. "I'm curious about that package," he said and got out. We followed him into the building and up to a counter. The sign over the counter said it was an air courier delivery service.

Warren flashed his badge and identified himself. "Special Agent Stevens, FBI. I need to see that package the man just dropped off."

The man behind the counter hesitated. "Look, I can talk to your supervisor about you accepting illegal drugs, or you can cooperate now. Your call."

The man reached in a bin and pulled out the package, carefully handing it to Warren as though it were a bomb. It was about a foot square and taped up well. Warren looked at the address and turned to us. "It's going to New Jersey, to one Carl Machavo. I know that name well. One of the drug kingpins in the Grisdella mob." He turned to the man who looked pale now and said, "I have to confiscate this package under Law Order 524, transporting illegal drugs. You were lucky you didn't send this out. Your company would be in deep doo-doo with us Feds." He signaled to us to leave. We did.

Back in the van Warren gave the package to Walt and said to store it. He said he'd give it to the Vegas FBI and let them handle it.

I asked, "What exactly is Law Order 524?"

186

"I have no idea, I just made it up." Warren snickered.

Walt checked his instruments and got us back on Fresard's travels. We drove out, navigated by Walt, and then the van stopped ahead. We pulled up to a safe distance to where we could see Fresard getting out of the van and into a car being driven by another man.

"Crap, he's losing the van. I'll see if we can follow," Warren said and then pulled binoculars from a console next to him. He called off the plate numbers as Walt wrote them down. Walt went to his computer, entered the numbers and hit a key. A few seconds later it spit out an owner of the vehicle. "Palermo Exports. It's a company car. It's also on the watch list for mob activities."

"Why do mobs always use import-export businesses? Dave asked.

"Easier to transport illegal goods and even humans," Trapper said. "When I was in the CIA, we had to deal with a few organizations that used export activities to send humans out through cargo ships. Mostly women."

"Any hookers?" I asked with a grin.

"I'll never tell."

Chapter 25

We once again followed Fresard, now with his new friend. Warren called to his men with the description of the car and its route and told them to keep a watch out. Suddenly some idiot cut us off, pulling in front of the van, forcing Warren to hit the brakes. The idiot wouldn't move. Warren was steaming and got out of the van. He went to the car and pulled his weapon. The person in the car looked like a stoner. He turned his head and saw Warren with the big .356 aimed at him.

"Move your damn vehicle or I'll blow holes in your head!" He held his badge up. "Then I'll arrest your dead body! Now get your ass out of the way!"

The man looked shocked and peeled out. Warren ran back to the van and moved forward. "Crap, I don't see the car now."

Dave was in the passenger seat. "I saw the car turn right up ahead. Maybe we can still find them."

Warren drove to the road and turned. The road was empty. No cars to be seen. "Damn, now what do we do?"

"See if any of your agents saw him. They seem to be everywhere," I said.

Warren got on his radio in the van and made a call to the other agents, asking if they had Fresard spotted. He got all negative reactions. We sat there waiting for anyone to report that Fresard was in the area.

~~*~~

The car pulled up to the building and Fresard got out. The mystery man followed Fresard to the door. Fresard stopped and turned to the man. "Louis, I want you to stay away from the lab. Do not go in there. Do you understand?"

The man stood staring at Fresard, then said, "Why can't I go see the new drug being made?"

"It's top secret, and if you knew anything about the process, I'd have to kill you," Fresard said.

"You want to keep this all to yourself, don't you? You went out on your own and now you want to have it all. When the Grisdellas arrive tomorrow, you'll be the king, won't you?"

"Are you crazy? No one holds it over the Grisdellas. They end up dead, like you're going to end up if you go anywhere near the lab. Do you understand?"

Campground Murders

Louis didn't say a word. Fresard unlocked the door and they went in. "Go through that door. There's a lounge in there with game machines and a TV. Keep yourself busy," Fresard said and waited for Louis to go to the door and in.

He turned and went into the lab. Harper was hovering over the equipment doing his thing. Fresard looked over at the women. They were sitting on the floor looking bored.

"Ass!" Penny yelled at the man.

He smiled and said, "You're lucky I'm keeping you alive. I need guinea pigs for the demonstration tomorrow. What better victims than a famous TV lady and a sheriff's wife? Adds an air of respectability."

"What makes you think we will take the drug?" Sarah yelled.

"Oh, you will take it. I'll have you strapped down to my special table," he said, pointing to what looked like a surgical table, complete with straps. "Now rest well. Tomorrow you will be famous for more than talking to celebrities. You'll be the first person in history to use a very new drug. People will revere you and it will be something to talk about on your show. If you survive." He laughed and went to Harper.

190

"So have you got a batch of it yet?"

Harper stopped what he was doing. "I can't rush it. This process is critical. I move too quickly and I ruin the whole thing. Do you want that?"

"Okay, professor, do your thing." Fresard moved away and then stopped. "Don't forget, Harper, if you don't cooperate, your bride will be dead." He left the lab as Harper stood looking at the samples he'd created, debating whether he should destroy the lab.

Penny stood and asked, "What did he mean, that he would kill your wife?"

"He has men holding my wife out in Brinnon. He will slowly murder her if I don't do this."

"Jeff, your wife is in police custody, under their protection. I know because her husband is the sheriff and he has her safe," Penny said, hoping Harper would believe her.

He stood looking at her. Sarah got up and said, "Jeff, believe her. I saw her before we were abducted. She's alive and well. Fresard put her in the hospital when he hit her on the head. She got out and has been watched by our deputies. She's not in any danger."

Campground Murders

Harper was quiet, then said, "It will be alright. Don't worry." Then he went back to work on the drug.

~~*~~

We were still waiting for word on the car. It was getting very late and no one had seen the vehicle. I was getting worried, not knowing if Penny and Sarah were even still alive. Warren cursed and started the van. He drove into the complex. It was huge and spread out over a good number of streets. He drove around, going between each building, looking. We saw nothing.

"I'm not even sure if the car came in this area," Warren said, stopping, then getting on his radio again and making another call for reports. No sightings.

My cell phone buzzed, and I saw it was Lynn. I answered, "Hey, what's up?"

"Jim, got a call from OCU that there is movement in the Grisdella family coming out here. They have a plane booked to arrive tomorrow morning around nine. This could have everything to do with the drug."

"Thanks, keep me informed. Maybe they will lead us to Fresard. Hopefully Penny and Sarah are still alive." I hung up and told the men what Lynn said.

Warren said, "At least Fresard still has this thing scheduled. If Harper has the formula in his head and Fresard is going to promote the thing, that should tell us Harper is still alive. Maybe Fresard is going to use the women for his demonstration. Then they would be still alive. If we can follow the mob from the airport to where Fresard is hiding out, we may be able to take down the Grisdellas and save the girls."

"It sounds good on paper, but will it work?" Dave asked with a smile. "I'm sure Sarah is playing along. She's no dummy. Plus Penny is smart. They'll be all right."

"We need to go back to my office and regroup. At this point either the women are alive or dead. But we need to stop Fresard and the mob," I said, hoping I wasn't right about the women being dead.

Warren started the van and drove out. We went back to the office and inside. Warren jumped when the back door cow bell rang. I laughed. "It's my secretary's alarm system. Works, too."

"It's loud. She should be able to hear it," he replied.

"Plus she's watching us on camera," I said as I pointed to the camera above us.

Campground Murders

"Do you have that much crime out here that you even need security surveillance?" Warren asked as we walked down the hall to the conference room.

"Talk to Buck about the security issues in Vegas. He has some stories to tell."

We entered the room. Lynn and Deacon were sitting at the table looking worn. I went to them. "Who has the baby?"

"Paula and Earl. They volunteered to watch her while we looked for our suspect and hostages," she said.

"I wondered what happened to Earl. I'll see he gets paid overtime. I wonder if he can change a diaper," I said with a smile.

"Paula can, I'm sure. So where do we stand now?" Lynn asked.

"I hate to say it, but we wait until tomorrow morning. Following the Grisdellas is our only chance at finding the location of Fresard. So far we've lost track of Fresard at every turn."

"I'm not going anywhere," Deacon said. "We all aren't."

"Thanks. You two are great friends," I said and went to Lacey who was sitting in the room. "Why don't you go home and get some sleep?" I suggested.

She looked up and said, "No way. When you find this guy, I want a piece of him. I'm staying. Tracey and I already set up the store room to sleep in."

I bent over, kissed her forehead and said, "Thanks."

*

Chapter 26

It was a very long night. Everyone was napping in their chairs and some managed to claim the couches in the lobby. I was in my office lying back in my desk chair. I had slept many times in this chair, but tonight I couldn't. My mind was still racing with thoughts of Penny. How many times had she been kidnapped but we usually found her quickly. This was the first time it was an overnight kidnapping, and I wasn't happy.

I reached for the remote for the TV and turned it on. Maybe a late night movie would bore me to sleep or at least take my mind off the women. Sarah was especially nice and got along well with Penny. I hoped they would both be all right. I wasn't a religious person, but I said a little prayer just in case. Amazing how we turn to the unseen deity when things look bleak. But it couldn't hurt as a backup.

There was a re-run of the "Bourne Identity." One of my favorite movies. I watched it for a while then got distracted. I shut it off and sat in the semi-darkness of the room. The only light came from a fake aquarium I had set up. It looked real but had fake fish. I felt a little foolish having it, but I didn't have time to take care of fish. Hell, I was hardly in my office, so taking care of fish wasn't on my list of priorities. I watched the fish sway in the water, attached to the strings holding them in place. They looked so peaceful. I wished I was held by a string, floating in water.

My door opened quietly and Dave looked in. He smiled when he saw I was awake.

"Come on in since we both can't sleep." I looked at my desk clock. It was almost four in the morning.

"I've been out wandering around your parking lot. Thinking. Sarah has been grabbed by psychos before. We always managed to save her quickly. Warren and Walt were always there for me back then. They are good friends. Just like you have here. I never saw such devotion to you and Penny like I've seen here. Fresard is second to every one finding Penny. And my Sarah. I don't know how to thank them."

"They don't want thanks. They will do what needs to be done and return our wives. They know we are thankful."

"Well, when this is over, I'm treating everyone to dinner," Dave said.

"And I know just the place," I said with a smile.

My door opened again and Deacon looked in. "Come on in, join the party," I said.

Deacon sat by the desk in my client chair. "It's quiet out there. Everyone can't sleep and we all want to get this operation going. But everyone is pretending to sleep."

"Well, we only have five hours. Hardly any time at all. Does Lynn have someone watching the airport for the flight in?"

"Yeah, three cars all ready to follow the car picking up the mob family. Plus Warren has about twenty cars all situated to follow also. We aren't going to lose them. There will be more security following them than when the President came to town," Deacon said.

Campground Murders

The door opened again and Trapper looked in. "Hell, just call everyone to come on in." I laughed.

He came in, pulled over a chair from beside the door, and sat. "So are we having a party and I wasn't invited?"

"If you can get a party out of the three of us, go for it," I said. I looked at Deacon. "Where's Lynn?"

"She slipped out to go see how the baby was doing. She'll be back shortly."

"Isn't this going to be hard on her, having to stake out and still want to be with the baby?" I asked.

"She's wondering where this will go. I don't think she wanted to retire, but she's been on the force for over fifteen years. Time to move on, I'd say."

"You just want her lieutenant slot. That's what you want."

"If they need someone to fill in for her, I won't argue," Deacon said with a smile.

"That's the one nice thing about being a sheriff, there's nowhere else to go. Unless you start as a deputy. I was thrown into the position straight out of the PD in Tacoma. So I didn't have to kill anyone off to get the job," Dave said.

Trapper said, "I moved up from patrolling the streets of Vegas on a bicycle to becoming a homicide detective as a lieutenant in Michigan. Then I gave that all up to be back in Vegas. Maybe I should get a bike to complete the cycle."

"I want to see you in those bike shorts the bike patrol cops wear. You have the legs for it." I laughed.

"You couldn't fit in the shorts. You need spanks."

"I couldn't fit in spanks either."

"Trapper, where's Warren?" Dave asked Trapper.

"Last I saw him, he and Walt were going out the back door. I didn't follow, so don't know where they went."

Dave smiled and said, "They're probably sleeping in the half million dollar van. They even have pull out cots in there."

We could hear the back door cowbell clang. I reached over to the small monitor on my desk and turned it on. I flipped the switch for the back door and I could see Lynn coming in. "Deacon, your wife is back."

Campground Murders

He smiled and stood. "Thanks, I'll go listen to her tell me how much she misses the baby." He turned to the door and went out.

"I went through the baby thing years ago. My son is now thirty-three. I have a daughter that I didn't know about. She appeared a couple months ago. She's great and I wish I had known about her years back." I was just talking out loud. "Dave, do you have any children?"

"None that I know about yet." He laughed. "Sarah and I have only been married a couple months so we are not rushing to have children yet."

"They can be a joy," I said as my door opened again. This time it was Lynn. I said, "You're going to be a wreck by morning."

"It's for a good cause," she replied. "I'm going to find a chair to crash on by the phones. Don't wake me unless it's an emergency." She smiled and went back out.

Dave said, "She's a homicide lieutenant?"

"Yep, we grow them big, attractive and dangerous down here," I said then laughed loudly. I needed that.

Bob Moats

~~*~~

Penny and Sarah were doing the best they could, trying to sleep next to each other on the cold cement floor. Penny looked at Sarah, still awake, and said, "I don't know how this will go, but it's been a pleasure knowing you."

"You, too. But I think we will be spending more time together when our husbands rescue us."

"I love your optimism. It's so refreshing. Not that I don't think my husband will rescue me, but he'll have the full force of the Las Vegas police behind him. You've only got the FBI helping your husband," Penny said with a laugh.

"Yes, and we know how inept they are. I wonder what Harper meant when he said we don't have to worry."

"I haven't any idea. I hope he knows what he's doing. I don't want to be a drug addled stoner, fighting to get a fix." Penny went silent for a moment. "I wonder what time it is."

Sarah looked at her watch and said, "It's just past six o'clock. I heard Fresard tell Harper that his demonstration is supposed to be around nine. Three more hours to wait. I don't know if I can hold out."

Campground Murders

"You'll make it. You're strong," Penny said.

"No, I mean I don't know if I can hold out. I need to use the bathroom," Sarah said.

"Oh, that's a different problem. Now that you mention it, I have to use the restroom also." They stood and started to yell loudly.

About five minutes later a door opened and in walked Fresard. "What the hell is wrong with you two? I need to sleep," he yelled.

"Yeah, well, we need to pee. Didn't you ever think we had to?" Penny yelled back at him. "There's no damn toilet in here."

He stood swaying and said, "So use the corner of the cage."

*

Chapter 27

"Are you nuts? Don't answer that, I already know," Penny yelled back at him. "Your visitors may not like smelling our waste products. Not a good image for your wonder drug."

Fresard stood with half-closed eyes. "Alright! One at a time and if the first one out gets cute, I'll kill the other. I only need one of you for the demonstration anyway." He went to the cage and unlocked it with a key from his pants pocket. He took the gun tucked in his belt and held it out. "Okay, who needs to go first?"

Penny told Sarah to go. She exited the cage and Fresard locked it back up. He led Sarah through a door leaving Penny alone. Harper was nowhere to be seen. She didn't remember Fresard taking Harper anywhere, so he must be still by the tables. Probably on a cot or the floor.

About five minutes later they returned and Penny took her turn. Fresard led her to a door in the hallway that had one of those uni-sex restroom signs on the door. She entered and looked around the room. It had no other exit and no windows. No way to escape, and if she tried, she'd put Sarah's life in danger. Penny did her business and came out. Fresard took her back to the cage.

"Now shut up and get some sleep," he barked at them and left the lab.

~~*~~

By seven-thirty we were all up and the adrenaline was flowing. Lynn had her people at the private terminals of McCarran Airport watching for the flight in. They'd report to the other spotters what type of car picked them up. They even had the stealth helicopter ready to fly.

I knew there were a dozen cars along the route ready to follow the car when it left the airport. As soon as all the mobsters were in the building we would go in. We discussed the options of attacking the place. With all the wiseguys in the room, they would be shooting at us. If Penny and Sarah were anywhere near, they would be ignored as we attacked. Carefully, though. Warren said they'd examine the situation when they got there and see if they had options.

I put my trust in these men. They were trained for this sort of thing.

Bob Moats

Lynn called to us as we sat in the conference room, "Got a call that the plane is landing in twenty minutes. My people are ready as well as the Feds. We won't lose them."

That was a long twenty minutes until the plane touched down. Lynn said that the Learjet taxied onto the tarmac in front of the terminal hangers. The spotters watched as a limo pulled around the building and stopped at the plane. One of the detectives had long range binoculars and gave Lynn the plate number.

We got the word that the car was there and it was a long black limo. That worried me. On any given day there was a flood of limos driving around Vegas. Weddings, partiers and celebrities would rent them and drive around the city. It would be easy for this limo to get lost in the rush. I had to trust the cops and agents who were watching for the car to keep it in sight.

The limo was loaded with eight men and was leaving the airport, moving onto the road. Lynn said her men were following, taking turns keeping behind the car.

Lynn was reporting where they were going. The limo pulled out on Russell Road and then turned north on Eastern Avenue. The unmarked Fed cars were still following. The limo turned on Tropicana

205

and went to the strip. Lynn looked at us and said, "I think they're sight-seeing."

~~*~~

Crap, I thought. We'd have to wait while those assholes took a tour of the city.

Fresard was pushing Harper to get ready for the demonstration. Harper was using a cot by the tables so Penny hadn't seen him.

"Is this going to be ready for the demo?" he yelled at Harper.

"It's ready now, stop yelling. I'm not fucking deaf," Harper yelled back.

Fresard was surprised by the outburst. He went silent and then said quietly, "Good. Now, the people will be here shortly. Put on a smile and do your best to promote this thing. There may even be a bonus in it for you." He turned and went to the cage.

"As for you two, decide who will be our victim...oops, I mean volunteer." He gave them an evil grin and left the lab.

"I'll do it. You're still young and have a life ahead of you. I'm sixty and I've done it all. You need to get on," Penny said.

206

Sarah didn't say anything right away. Then, "I'm sure we'll both be rescued before that happens."

"Doesn't matter. If they are late, I'll still go, and I don't want to hear any arguments or I'll clock you," she said with a slight grin.

The door burst open and Fresard came back in with Louis. "Do those jerks think that I have all the time in the world to screw around? They're taking a sight-seeing tour of Vegas. Wasting my time! Damn it!" He stormed over to the first lab table and grabbed a glass, ready to throw it. Then he stopped and set it back down. He calmed and said, "Go watch the parking lot for their arrival. Bring them in here as soon as they arrive."

Louis went back out the door and Fresard turned to Harper, standing behind him. "We are being stalled by small minds. I'll see to it these men are all brought down. I'll take over the whole operation with this drug. So do good and I'll make you rich."

"What about my wife?" Harper asked.

Fresard was taken off guard. "She'll live. Don't worry." He left the lab.

Penny called to him, "He lied to you about your wife, he'll lie to you about making you rich. He'll take the formula and go off after killing you and us."

Campground Murders

Harper watched Penny for a moment. "Whoever he chooses to try the drug, don't worry." He went back to work, moving his equipment around.

Penny looked at Sarah and said, "He said it again. I'm not even going to ask. I don't think he's going to tell."

~~*~~

Warren, Walt, Dave, Trapper and I got into the FBI van and waited for Lynn to get word of the arrival. I instructed Warren where to go to get to the area where we suspected they would be. Closer to the source.

We parked in a lot for some electronic manufacturing company and waited. Walt relayed info to us from Lynn. She said they were up by the Stratosphere but turning around, going south on the strip. I hoped they were coming back.

We sat for what seemed to be a year before we saw a long black limo drive past us. Lynn called and said they had entered the complex. Walt called back that we had it in sight. Warren got on the phone and said, "Have your men hang back until we can get a take on the scene. I'll call when we need help. Hopefully we can resolve it peacefully."

We heard Lynn say, "Forget peaceful, shoot the bastards." Then we heard her laugh. Warren handed the phone back to Walt and got back into the driver's seat. He started the van and drove out slowly, still watching the limo as it cruised the area.

"Maybe they don't know where to go," Dave said.

"I'm sure the driver has directions. These limo people are good," I said.

We kept our distance as the limo slowed and then turned on the next street. Warren hung back, figuring the driver wouldn't feel like he was being followed. But Warren was being cautious. He pulled up to the street, and we could see the limo pull into a parking lot by a small building. Walt reported the landing of the limo as we drove down the street.

Warren pulled into the parking lot of the building next to the one in question and we got out. Walt had opened a case in the van that had all kinds of weapons. Warren wanted the scatter gun. Dave took an Uzi-type gun. I had my Glock so I was fine with it. Trapper wanted the AK-47. Macho man he was. I was surprised they had a Russian weapon, but didn't ask.

We watched as three Fed cars came down the road. Walt waved to them from the drive to the parking lot. They pulled in and Warren gathered them as they got out of their cars.

"Okay, all of you hang back here until I signal you." He pulled his walkie-talkie out and tested it. The team leader said it worked.

Warren looked at us and said, "Let's go see where the party is."

*

Chapter 28

We went around the building to the one in question. It was a small factory and had very few windows. Probably for the offices, and they were covered from the inside. There were two cars in the parking lot, one the limo and the other was the one Fresard came in yesterday. We stood behind bushes watching the building when another car pulled in.

"Great, more bad guys," Warren said.

Four men got out and went into the building. Warren said to follow. He ran down the side of our building and over to the back of the one we wanted. Dave said, "There's some windows in the top of the factory that we may be able to see in."

Bob Moats

Warren saw a metal ladder leading up to the roof of the lower part of the building. From there they could get to the windows. Warren said it was good. "Walt, stay here so I can let you know on the radio what we see."

I said I would wait on the ground. I knew my weight and dislike of heights would keep me off the roof. Trapper said he'd stay with me. Dave and Warren climbed the ladder to the roof and stood on a box-like housing, probably for air-conditioning. They carefully looked in the windows.

Warren radioed back to Walt that they could see Penny and Sarah. My heart jumped a bit. Warren said there were eleven people in the large room, and there was a door to the outside on the parking lot side of the building.

While they watched, Warren explained what was going on. "Fresard is going to where Penny and Sarah are locked in a cage. He's opening it and taking Penny out. They're taking her to a table. Now they are strapping her down. Okay, call the men in. We have to stop this."

Warren and Dave came down fast.

~~*~~

"Okay, gentlemen, our volunteer is going to be injected with the drug so you can see firsthand what it does." He signaled to Harper to begin. Harper went to Penny with a syringe. Leaning over her, he whispered, "Don't worry. Just act like you're high."

Penny suddenly figured out what he meant. He wasn't injecting her with the drug. She didn't like needles but waited until Harper had finished. She struggled a bit then went limp. She acted like she was on a trip in an old sixties movie.

"What's wrong with her?" the boss of the mob men asked. "She looks like she's having a bad trip."

Penny realized she was over acting and settled down, making little noises that sounded like a kitten purring.

Suddenly they heard a loud noise, an explosion.

~~*~~

Walt had stuck explosives on the outer door to the factory floor, and it blew off the hinges. All of Warren's men streamed in, firing at the men inside who started firing back. I came up the rear as I saw Harper unstrapping Penny from the table. One of the hoods came up behind Harper and was going to fire, but I shot him with my Glock. I amazed myself that I hit him. Harper took Penny back by the cage and they lay down low to the ground.

Bob Moats

The gun fire continued as the hoods were dropping. The Feds had body armor which helped them. I saw one big man running to another door. He was too well dressed to be a wiseguy, he had to be the boss. I yelled to Warren, pointing them out. He waved and went after the men. I came around just behind Dave as he went to the cage. I was giving us cover by firing back, although no one was really shooting at us. They were busy with the Feds.

Dave yelled to Sarah to get back as he fired on the lock, blowing it off the cage with the Uzi. He opened the door and Sarah came out. She wanted to grab onto Dave but he said to wait. We went to Harper and Penny. I helped my wife up, and we all went to the door on the side.

Dave said, "Let the Feds fight it out. We need to get to safety." We went through the door and down the hall. I turned to see if anyone was following. No one was. The gun fire continued. The hoods weren't giving up and the Feds were going to stop them.

We went to an opening to the lobby of the building and took the women and Harper to sit on the couches. I stood watching the hall, waiting for any of them to come through the factory door. Suddenly a side door opened. Dave and I brought our weapons up and waited. It was Warren. He smiled at us and said, "Now that's what I call a party."

213

Campground Murders

The gun fire had ceased, and the lead agent called to Warren on the radio, saying the area was secured. More than half of the bad guys were dead and the rest were being loaded in a prisoner step van provided by LVMPD. Lynn came in from the back and gave Penny a hug.

"I knew you guys wouldn't desert us," Penny said to Lynn. She introduced Sarah to Lynn and they shook hands.

Warren had Harper on the couch, talking to him. I went over to get away from the women gabbing. Warren was questioning Harper about his involvement in this drug situation. I stood next to Dave as we listened to him explain about how he got to this point.

"After the women told me that Fresard didn't actually have my wife, I played along until help could arrive. I injected Mrs. Wickens with saline water. I wasn't going to get her into the drug."

I said thanks for that. He looked at me blankly. I said, "I'm Mr. Wickens."

He smiled and continued, "Fresard was going to get some backing then take over the mob family, forcing them out once he had enough of the drug ready to push."

214

"Well, no one is going to take over anything now. The agency will want to talk to you about the drug and its potential. The FDA may even get involved especially if this drug were to become something of a problem."

Everyone was gathering in the parking lot as Warren, Dave and I thanked them for a good bust. Not one agent was injured or killed. Lynn had the hoods taken to the precinct for transfer to a federal facility for processing on charges of drug distribution and kidnapping. Harper was taken to the Vegas bureau of the FBI for questioning about his involvement. I felt sorry for him once Penny explained her feelings. I was sure his bride back in Brinnon would be happy to hear he was still alive. Dave called Mike, told him to tell her, and asked how the dogs were.

Dave told us that Willy and Van Gogh were fine and at the station. "Oh, and your stew is finished." Dave laughed as he told the girls.

An hour later we were back in the office, resting. The FBI agents had all gone back to the Bureau office, and the cops had all gone back to their jobs. Lynn and Deacon gave their apologies and went to get their baby from Earl and Paula. Trapper went off to do his thing and Buck was getting his men back to their guarding duties after I thanked them for their part in helping to try and find the suspect.

Campground Murders

Warren, Walt, Dave, Sarah, Penny and I sat relaxing on our couches in the lobby. Lacey was bouncing around, happy that everyone was safe.

"So what's going to happen to Harper?" Sarah asked.

"He'll be questioned, and they may arrest him for something just to make an example out of him. He probably won't do much time if any at all. His only crime was trying to sell the formula. They may go easy on him for helping Penny and Sarah. He was a victim, too."

"Hey, we haven't eaten since yesterday," Penny said. "Let's go attack Angelo's then Dave and Sarah can meet our daughter."

Sounded good to me. We got up, I told Lacey to close up and we went out. Then we realized that our cars were still back in Brinnon. Warren said, "All of us can fit into the van if we double up on the seats." I looked over to the cute cars Buck bought for the security guards and said to wait. I went back in and got the keys from Buck to one of the cars then came back out.

"Warren, follow me in the van," I said, and took Dave and Sarah to the car.

*

Chapter 29

Angelo was happy to see us and took us to our usual table. The best in the house. We sat as I introduced everyone to Angelo and asked him if Carol was working.

"Sure, Mr. R, she's in back. Want to see her?"

"Just for a few minutes, I'd appreciate it."

"I'll get her," he said and went off.

I looked at our guests and said, "Angelo is the son of a mafia princess, or I should say Queen. His stepfather is Gino Traviano."

Warren gave me a stare. "He's son of one of the mafia family capos in New York? How do you know him?"

"It's a long story, but he's on our side, and our good friend. I'll tell you about it on the way back to Brinnon."

Carol came out to our table. "Hey, Dad, Mom. I thought you were going on vacation."

Campground Murders

"We were, long story, I'll fill you in later." I introduced her to our new friends.

"So, I'll make sure you get a meal to remember," she said and went back to the kitchen.

We sat talking about our lives and then had our meal. It was great.

We finished and said our good-byes to Angelo and Carol then went out to our home. It was strange not having Willy around. But he was safe back in Brinnon. We set up Walt and Warren in our spare room and let Dave and Sarah have the guesthouse. Everyone was happy.

Later that night we relaxed out back. Of course, Penny got Sarah into the pool. Warren, Walt, Dave and I sat drinking plenty of beer and talking about our adventures in crime fighting. As it was getting dark, I took everyone out to the front of the house. I wanted to show them the lights of the strip. It was a warm beautiful night and the strip was glowing.

We were all wearing down. It had been a long two days. So we said our good nights and went to our rooms. I cuddled with Penny, and she told me she was thankful for all good people in our lives.

"We are lucky to be where we are. I wouldn't trade this for anything," I said.

The night was still, and I slept well. The next morning we got up. Penny and Sarah attempted breakfast. It wasn't too bad, so we ate it.

The men gathered out front as we tried to figure the ride back. The van didn't really have enough room for all of us driving eighteen hours. Buck came driving up and parked. I was glad to see him. I had an idea.

I took Buck aside and explained the situation. He laughed. "I'd love a road trip. I've always wanted to see the Pacific Northwest. When do we leave?"

"I'm figuring early tomorrow morning. Give our guests time to see a little of Vegas. You can drive us in the mini-limo then drive it back while Penny and I drive our motorhome."

"That works for me. Tell me when you need me and I'll bring some things to take with me."

"Thanks, Buck. I owe you."

We went back to the men and explained what my plan was.

"That'll work. Walt and I can take our van and you guys go in your vehicle. Shall we tell the women?" Warren said.

Campground Murders

We spent the rest of the day exploring Vegas. Penny took Sarah to the Boulevard Mall while the men went to the Flamingo casino to lose a little money. Walt came away with about two thousand dollars in winnings. Warren, Dave and I barely broke even.

"I'm sure the little genius cheats somehow," Warren said about Walt and his winnings.

The next morning early, around 5 a.m., Buck arrived. I pulled the mini-limo out of the garage and gave Buck the keys. I wanted to be in back with Dave, Sarah and Penny. I told Warren that the limo was a present from the Traviano family for saving their niece. He was impressed with the vehicle.

We all got into our respective vehicles and left Vegas, going on the road again. I never thought I'd travel so much in so short a time. We all took turns driving to make the trip a little easier, and we made good time.

We drove straight through since we weren't sightseeing, just getting back to where we left off. Warren had to get back to his office to file a ton of reports, and Dave needed to be sure Virgil and Mike didn't let crime run rampant on the streets.

Mike called and said that the Seattle FBI picked up Mrs. Harper and drove her and her car to Vegas to meet her husband. They decided to let Harper skate on charges in exchange for his testimony on illegal behavior by Emerson Pharmaceuticals. He would be out of work, but I heard later from Warren that a rival drug company wanted him to work for them.

We arrived back in Brinnon around ten that night and went to the sheriff's office. We stretched our legs and went into the station. I yelled for Willy as we came to the counter, but he didn't come running. I looked past the counter and saw him sleeping with Van Gogh on the floor. He was curled up close to the big dog.

Penny saw him and called. He perked up and saw us, then bolted up and ran around the counter to us. Penny picked him up, and he licked her face fiercely.

Mike came forward to the counter. "Dave, the Feds picked up Mrs. Harper around three and took her away. That woman was sure happy to hear you guys found her husband." Mike's jaw dropped when he saw Buck come up behind us. He had that effect on people.

"Mike, this is our friend and my business associate Buck Carson. Is Virgil around?" I asked.

"Nope, he went home to sleep. He's coming back around eleven to take my place. Good to meet you, Buck." They shook hands.

Campground Murders

Dave asked, "Any crimes to report?"

"Nope, it's been real peaceful since you've been gone. What shall we do with Laymen's car?"

"Call his wife and see if she wants us to bring it to her in Olympia. You and Virgil can take it tomorrow." Dave turned to us and said, "Now it's late and we need to go home to see if the stew is worth eating or throwing out."

Sarah laughed and said, "Why don't we take our guests for a fancy dinner at the Halfway House?"

Dave laughed and said to us, "Okay, it's more of a burger joint but the food is good."

"Sounds good," Penny and I agreed.

Outside the office Warren told us that he and Walt were going to head back to Seattle.

"Jim, Penny, it's been a pleasure to know you, even if you are friends with the mob." He gave us a big smile. "If you make it up to Seattle, call and I'll give you a tour." He handed me his card and they said their good-byes. Walt and Warren got into the van and drove out.

"So, shall we go eat?" I offered the limo to go there. They liked that idea. Dave and I sat in front while Buck, Penny and Sarah sat in back with the dogs.

We pulled into the restaurant and parked. There were a few people in the lot watching us get out. They knew Dave and Sarah and asked if they came into some money.

Dave called back, "We just got back from Vegas. Made a fortune at slots." He laughed and said to me, "That will be all over town by midnight."

We went in, and it was the same in there. Everyone was questioning Dave on his ride. He played it up big for the people. I was trying not to laugh.

We had a good meal and then left. We drove by the General Store to retrieve Sarah's car, and Dave drove it back to their house. Sarah and Penny took all the wine out of Sarah's car and into the house. I let Willy run the yard with Van Gogh as Dave and I stood watching the dogs run.

"Good to be home," Dave said. I agreed.

We went in and settled in the living room. Buck was in love with the house, so Sarah took him on a tour. Dave brought out beers for him and me, and we relaxed in the night.

*

Chapter 30

Next morning Buck announced that he was driving back. "Are you going to be alright by yourself?" I asked.

"I'm not rushing back. I may stop halfway down for a night. I know a nice lady in Redding, California. I may stop to say hi." He gave us his walrus smile, and I said to be careful.

We watched him drive off and then Penny and I went to our van. It felt good to be back in the thing. Penny put all the packages she bought into the back bedroom. I just smiled.

Dave came to the door and peeked in. "Hello, anyone home?"

I went to the door and said, "Penny is trying to pack all her new stuff. I'm glad this isn't a plane. We'd never get off the ground." I suddenly felt a whack on my back. Penny was behind me.

I stepped out of the van as Sarah came up. Penny joined us.

"Hate to see you go. It's been a fun few days," Sarah said.

"Fun?" I said. "You and Penny were kidnapped and taken a thousand miles from your home and locked in a cage, subjected to dangerous people and barely lived to tell."

"Yes, fun. We could have sat around here talking about the weather. Do you have to leave?"

"Penny has a show to get ready for, and we still need to see Seattle before going back. I enjoyed our stay in your front yard although Penny didn't get to roast marshmallows."

"Next time you come back, we will. I hope you do," Sarah said.

Penny hugged Sarah and said we would. We got into the van, making sure Willy was with us. We waved and drove out the long drive.

"I'm going to miss them. I feel bad now that we didn't get to spend more quality time with them," Penny said with sadness in her voice.

I looked in the rearview mirror. I could see Dave and Sarah standing with Van Gogh, watching us go. I stopped the van and looked at Penny, "Do we really need to climb the Space Needle?"

Campground Murders

"Oh, hell, no," she said.

"Good, I didn't want to either," I said and put the van in reverse.

THE END.

For every ending there is a new beginning.

~~*~~

The following is a preview of the 26th book "Network Murders"

Prologue

Percy Isham sat at his desk poring over the new season's television schedule, trying to balance the shows. There were formulas for what shows followed another and at what times of the day. He was studying the daytime lineup and trying to decide where to balance the second run shows around the new talk show. Well, Penny Wickens' talk show was not new to this network. Three years ago, they had her show running until that serial killer started to murder her guests. Her show was pulled off the air, but the killer threatened to murder more people if she wasn't put back on. They yielded to his demands and the situation went bad until that private eye and his buddies managed to stop the killer.

However, Penny Wickens used her contractual option to leave her show. She was not happy with the way the network handled the situation and they lost a ratings gold mine. Now they got her back, and it was going to be a big celebration when her show premiered next week. They spent a lot of money on advertisements to promote the show. This time it was from Las Vegas, another ratings winner.

They wanted the show to go on earlier but Wickens and her husband needed a couple weeks to take a vacation before getting back into it. She had now returned to Vegas and they had everything ready for her debut.

Isham sat in his office in Vegas, since he was the west coast head of programming. He opted to leave LA and settle in Vegas for many reasons. One was gambling, another was celebrities for the pickings to put in his shows.

It was nine in the evening. He liked to work late then go gambling. He finished his changes in the lineup and was happy with his decisions. The casinos awaited him and the bevy of women who knew him and wanted to bed the man who could put them on

Campground Murders

TV. Not that he really could get them a shot on television, but he led them to believe that.

He put everything safely away and went to the door of his office. He was alone in the building, the way he liked it. Less headaches dealing with people. He opened the door and was confronted by a dark figure in the outer room. He was startled.

"How did you get in here and who are you?" he asked.

The figure didn't respond, but came forward to the man. In the light of Isham's office he could see the stranger's face clearly.

"What the hell are you doing in here? I told you that I was not going to have any further dealings with you. I'm calling the police if you don't leave right now," Isham said.

It was the last words Percy Isham would ever speak as the figure brought up a gun and fired at the man.

*

Continued in the book...

Bob Moats

~~*~~

Jim Richards Family of Readers

Thanks to the following people who are now part of the Jim Richards Family of Readers. They have read a book or more and enjoyed them. They all volunteered to be included in the list. If you are a fan of the books, send me your full name and you will be included in future books. Send your name to murdernovels@bobmoats.com to be added here and on the website. (updated 3-30-14)

* Achim Feifel * Al Norris * Alex Wheatley * Alexandra Delporte-Wilkinson * Amy Tapia * Andrea Bryan * Anne Shepherd * Arianda Sugar * Arlene Markowski * Ashley Augustus * Audra Hall * Barbara Hughes * Barbara Sammons * Barbara Schuler * Barbara Zirger * Beth Donohue Plenskofski * Betsy Childress * Beth Gibson * Bill Sandy * Bill Tornquist * Billie-jo Collie * Boni J Rychener * Carl Bishopric * Carla Lewis * Carole Henderson * Carolyn Conroy * Carolyn Riddle-Linington * Cassy Bailey * Chad Hudson * Charlotte L Duran * Cheryl L. Everett * Cindy Ackley Nunn * Cindy Valstad * Connie Bancroft * Corinne Kay O'Daniel * Dana Robbins Chuchran * Dana Wichita * Danielle Monique * Darren

Campground Murders

Heald * Dave Travers * David Wilkinson * DeAnn Jannereth * Deanna Miller * Deb Breuker Balbo * Debbie Carter * Debbie White * Deborah Fartuch * Deborah Gauze * Deborah Sullivan * Dee King * Denise Freeman * Diana Carver * Dixie Beck * Donna Gould * Donna Thompson * Donny Minter * Doris Kight * Eddie Moore * Eric Walters * Felicia Annette Bradfield * Francine Menor * Gail Chesney * Georgiann Minster * George Conner * Greg Colucci * Hayley Rankin * Harold Garcia * Heidi Arnold * Irma Ranee Coy * Jacqueline Moss * Jan Kimball * Janice Schneider * Janice Spoor * Jennifer Redmond * Jessica Keown-Belous * Jim Beck * Jo Boguslaw * Jo Turner * Joanne Marie Turner * John Peiffer * John Wisbiski * Joseph Wauro * Joyce Stacy * Joyce Trifiletti * Judy Franklin * Judy Travers * Judy Padgett * Julie Heath * Junnahvee Benson * Karen Dahl * Karen Grams * Karen Higham * Karen Kaiser * Karen Meinburg Richwine * Karen Kirkman Parker * Karin Hawkins * Karin Vasvari * Kathleen Donohue Roesing * Kathleen Riddle-Wolfe * Kathy Hinds Moore * Kathy Jones * Kathy Mitchell * Katie Benzler * Kay Burns * Kelly Garcia * Ken Boggs * Keota Rodriguez * Kiera Mccarthy * Kim Estes * Kitty Stolle * Kristie Sciler * Kirsty Stanton * LaLonnie Scallen * Larry Morris * Leann Parr * Lenora Scales * Leslie Marie Jackson * Linda Forester * Linda Ingle Cox * Linda Kennerö * Linda Magill * Lisa Bower * Liz Gibson * Lorraine Wiman * Loretta Alexander * Lynda Bowles * Lynette Lawrance * LuAnn Louttit * Manny Rothman * Marcia Gibson DeWitt * Marie Calder * Marlene Bryan * MaryLouise Kramp * Mary Lynn Gross * Megan Atkins * Meghan Hyden * Melody Cannavan * Michael Carruthers * Michael Dinkens * Michael Vannoy * Michelle Burns-Mitchell * Michelle Pilcher * Micki Potter * Mike Moats * Mimi Baur * Myrna Hecht * Nadine Sutton * Natalie

Bob Moats

Quine * Neena Martin * O'Della Wilson * Pat Pollington
* Pat Rohn * Patricia Jarmon * Patricia C Trezza * Patrick
Barry * Paul Lawrance * Peggy Davis * Phyllis Bassett *
Raylene Matheny * Rebecca Collins Besner * Renee
Brumley * Reta Hanna * Reta Moats * Roberta Navarro-
Harder * Sally Berneathy * Sally Hubler * Sarah Santos *
Satka Nikc * Sharon E. Edwards * Sharon Mangini *
Sharon McMillon * Sheena Rawl * Sherry Amstutz *
Shirley Alvarez * Shirley Davies * Shirley Williams *
Stacie Rowe * Stephanie Conner * Steve Cullen * Susan
Haughton * Susan Hesse Adams * Susan Salomon *
Suzan K Chase * Taisha Cullum * Tamara Moore *
Tammy Castleberry * Tammy Lynn Wood * Ted Murphy
* Terri Atkins * Terri Creech * Terry Raab * Tonia
Rachael Riggs-Williams * Travis Fleury-Lopez * Twyla
Gawlas * Val Brooks * Walt Munsel * Yvonne Isakson *

Thank you to all these wonderful people.

Thank you for purchasing this book. I hope
you enjoy it as much as I enjoyed writing it
for my faithful readers. Please feel free to
email me to tell me what you thought about
my stories. I love hearing from the readers. I
can be reached at
murdernovels@bobmoats.com thanks again!

*

www.ingramcontent.com/pod-product-compliance
Lightning Source LLC
Chambersburg PA
CBHW070618130626
46556CB00001B/399